out on good

BEHAVIOR

DAHLIA ADLER

OUT ON GOOD BEHAVIOR
Copyright © 2016 by Dahlia Adler
Cover design: Maggie Hall
Interior formatting: Cait Greer

ISBN-10: 0-9909168-3-9 (e-book)
ISBN-13: 978-0-9909168-3-3

ISBN-10: 0-9909168-5-5 (paperback)
ISBN-13: 978-0-9909168-5-7

Other books by Dahlia Adler

The Radleigh University Series
Last Will and Testament
Right of First Refusal

The Daylight Falls Series
Behind the Scenes
Under the Lights

Just Visiting

To Queer Twitter,
the best of all the Twitters

chapter one

I've been betrayed.

To the left of me in our blue-velvet-lined booth at Delta, Lizzie Brandt is actually fucking *giggling* at whatever Connor, her boyfriend of nearly a year—a *year*—is whispering in her ear while she sips from a highball of scotch.

On my right, Cait Johannssen is trash talking about some sort of sports...thing, which is totally typical except that she's doing it with her fingers laced through *her* boyfriend Mase's.

And I...I'm the lone wolf.

Okay, I'm not that lone—Mase brought a couple of friends to the club from the Radleigh University basketball team, and one's left hand is about three inches from learning that I'm au natural under this dress—but still. *Boyfriends.* Serious ones. Who even does that?

1

"So, Frankie." I jolt to attention at the sound of my name, and realize Connor's spoken it, and now everyone's looking at me. "I hear congratulations are in order."

"For what?"

Cait snorts. "Only you wouldn't even blink at the fact that you're getting a whole freaking exhibit at an art show."

"Oh, right. That." I feel a little blush coming on and take a quick sip of my vodka martini. "It's not a big deal. I had stuff up at the last show, too."

"Yeah, but you didn't have your own *exhibit*," Lizzie says firmly, raising her glass in the air and nearly sloshing it over her hand. I'm not sure whether it's her third drink or her fourth, but she has definitely entered the "proud, cheerful drunk" portion of her evening, which is my favorite Lizzie phase. "This is huuuuge. We should have a party at the apartment to celebrate. Let's have a party!"

"We've been back at school for thirty seconds," says Cait, taking a sip from the single light beer she's been working on all night. She's on a hardcore campaign to win the lacrosse captainship that should've been hers this year, and cleaner living is factoring into that in a major way, sadly for the rest of us. "You're already party planning?"

"Hey, I declared a major—"

"Yeah, one you got lucky as fuck accepted a bunch of your random classes toward it," Cait reminds her.

"Whatever—you're just jealous because Cultural Studies is about sixty-nine times cooler than Econ." Lizzie takes another sip of her drink. "Anyway, I declared a major, I have the perfect resume-building part-time job this semester, my brothers are doing great, and I actually still like this one," she says, jutting her thumb in Connor's direction. "Even you're getting laid, Caity J! What's not to celebrate?"

Cait plucks a peanut from the little bowl in front of us and tosses it at Lizzie. It smacks off Lizzie's nose and bounces right into her scotch. "Ew, Cait!"

"My girl's still got it," Mase says fondly, nuzzling her neck.

"Fucking jocks," Lizzie mutters, taking another sip of her drink, peanut and all.

"Hey," Guy-with-his-hand-on-my-thigh chimes in with mock indignation. I'd actually kind of forgotten he was there.

"Yes?" Lizzie asks, blinking.

He doesn't respond, and the rest of us crack up laughing, though Mase quickly cuts himself off to flash a sympathetic smile instead.

"Now that I think about it," says Cait, "a party isn't such a bad idea. Seems like a good excuse to drag Samara out of the room."

The mention of Cait's roommate makes me perk up in my seat. "Samara, huh? Yeah, I'm definitely on board with this party."

"Oh God, stop it," Cait begs, throwing a peanut at me this time. "For the billionth time, Samara is the literal top of the no-touching list."

"Is she even gay?" Mase asks.

"No," Lizzie answers at the same time I say, "Yes."

Connor and Mase look between us, confused. Mase's friend's hand freezes on my thigh. "Wait, are *you*?"

"I don't discriminate by gender or lack thereof," I say, because sometimes, you just know "I'm pansexual" is going to be met with "What's that?" followed by "Isn't that just bi?" and finally "So, you're down for a threesome?"

This guy is definitely *that* guy.

He blinks, and I can already feel him pulling back, but whatever. I turn to the others. "I'm telling you, that girl likes girls. I swear, I will prove it by Spring Break."

"Please, no one take her up on that challenge," Cait pleads.

"Sorry, Cait," says Lizzie, "but you know I need to see how far Frankie's rainbow magic extends. I think we should put money on this one."

"You're *not* putting money on Frankie nailing my roommate."

Connor scratches his scruffy jaw. "That does seem to go a little beyond crass and into the realm of…"

"Lizzie-esque?" Cait fills in.

He smirks and says nothing, lifting his beer to his lips and taking a long drink.

"Why didn't she come tonight, anyway?" asks Mase.

"She doesn't have ID," says Cait. "Doesn't drink. Hence a house party would be a way better choice for her, and frankly, I think she could use something, stat. She did *not* come back from South Carolina this summer a happy camper."

"I can imagine," I murmur, taking a sip from my glass. If there's one thing I definitely remember from my few conversations with Samara last semester, it's that she and her family—most specifically her Republican politician father—don't mesh very well. Lizzie's right that Samara has never said a word to suggest she likes girls, but I've historically had pretty stellar gaydar, and it still pings every time I talk to her.

Or maybe I'm just flirting hard enough for both of us. It's been known to happen.

"So, party? Friday night?" Lizzie suggests. "Tell your friends! I'd tell mine, but, well." She gestures around the table.

The rest of us try not to snort with laughter and fail. Lizzie hasn't exactly made herself the best-liked student at Radleigh University—fooling around with a taken fraternity president and hooking up with a TA who nearly loses his job over it aren't really "Miss Popularity" plays—but God bless her, she doesn't seem to mind.

"Sounds good to me," I say cheerfully, imagining seeing Samara again in the comfort of my apartment. Just because I can't touch doesn't mean I can't look.

Just then, a familiar pair of long brown legs walks in, and I down the rest of my martini and stand up. Racquel I'm-Sure-She-Has-a-Last-Name-Somewhere is always good for a dance on the floor, followed by a dance in the women's bathroom, and all this talk of a girl I can't have has gotten me very in the mood for a girl I can. "Speaking of potential party guests, I'll…see you guys in a bit," I say, popping open my glittery clutch for a Tic Tac.

Lizzie follows my eye line to Racquel and groans. "Oh, great. That's the girl I'm talking about when I say 'the Loud One,'" she says to Connor in what isn't nearly as quiet a whisper as she thinks it is.

"Guess we're staying at my place tonight," he replies as I make my way over to where Racquel is looking pretty damn good in a clingy red dress under which I'm guessing she's wearing as little as I am.

"Count on it," I call back over my shoulder. Samara Kazarian may not be certain about who or what she wants, but I sure as hell am.

chapter two

"I'm here I'm here I'm here I'm here," I pant as I slide into my seat just as the clock hits eleven. Or maybe 11:01, judging by the way my brand-new art history professor is glaring at me over her glasses. "Sorry about that."

"And you are?"

"A little late but won't let it happen again?"

There are scattered titters around the classroom, and her face relaxes into a smile. "Well played."

I doff an imaginary cap.

She returns to addressing the class as a whole, which is probably about forty students. I recognize a few, but this is only my second art history class; most of my art focus is in Studio, and between that, core classes, and my Gender and Sexuality minor, I haven't had a whole lot of time to reach outside. I'm thrilled when I lock eyes with Abe Sutter, though—he and I have been in Studio together since freshman year, when we realized we were both eye-fucking the shit out of the same male model.

A syllabus lands on my desk with "Professor Paula Richter" and "Women in Visual Arts" printed at the top, and I immediately scan it to see whether there are any group projects so I can nab Abe as quickly as humanly possible. I don't see any, but I *do* see a field trip planned to an exhibit at the Met.

A thrill runs through me at the idea of going back to the museum for the first time in years, and judging by the murmuring going on around me, I'm not the only one who's noticed. "As it sounds like you've observed, yes, we'll be going on a class field trip to the Metropolitan Museum of Art in New York City. That's going to be an overnight trip on a weekend; if that's a problem with your schedule, please see me after class today."

Considering that since Lizzie and Cait paired off, I usually spend my Saturdays lying on my ass watching *Pawn Stars* while I sketch stuff for the online store that helps pay for my tattoos and social life. I'm definitely down for a weekend excursion, especially to the city.

"Ditto if anyone needs help financing the trip," Professor Richter continues. "Unfortunately, this trip isn't subsidized by the university, and I know the price tag might be a little steep for some of you, so if you require financial assistance, let's talk after class."

According to the syllabus, the estimated cost per student is a hundred bucks, not counting food, which *is* a little steep. I'm lucky enough to have my parents covering my textbooks, tuition, and rent, but I know that already pushes them to their limit. Still, I don't want to ask for financial assistance from Richter when I know there are plenty of kids in the class on loans who need it way more than I do.

I slip my phone out of my bag and check my bank balance. *Shit.* I'm down to six hundred bucks, the final remains of my summer earnings after paying for repairs to my Vespa and replacing my favorite squirrel-hair brush. Utilities will suck up half of that, and food will wreak havoc on the rest. I have a couple of commissions lined up through my website, but that only brings in another fifty. There's no question about it—I need to increase my cash flow.

For the rest of the lecture, I force all thoughts of finances out of my head and listen to Professor Richter talk about female sculptors in ancient Greece and Rome, but as soon as the bell rings, I race out of the room, phone in hand. *Emergency,* I text Cait. *I need a job, ASAP. Help a girl out with her resume?*

Sure, she writes back immediately. *As long as you can come over here. Practice wiped me out today.*

"Hey, Franklin!"

I turn with a smile as Abe greets me with my familiar nickname and we engulf each other in a huge bear hug. "Hey, handsome. So psyched you're in this class! Are you Tuesday and Thursday night Studio too?"

"I am! If we were gonna get sick of each other, we'd probably have done that by now, right?"

"I think so, but just to be sure, sit your ass next to me in this class from now on, will you?"

"Ahem, I believe *you're* the one who strolled in late and charmed the pants of the professor," he reminds me as we start walking in the direction of Cait's dorm. "No wonder you're rolling in more ass than you can handle."

"Bite your tongue." I slip my phone back into my pocket and shift the strap of my messenger bag so it lies flat between my boobs. "There's no such thing as more ass than I can handle. But speaking of which, how's it going with Fire Island Guy?" Abe and I didn't keep in touch a ton over break, but judging by the pictures he was posting online all summer, he was having quite the adventure.

"What happened on Fire Island is definitely staying on Fire Island," he says, shaking his head. "Hot guy, but holy shit—dumb as bricks."

"The cute ones always are," I say with a sigh. "You coming to the Rainbow House party?"

"Monday night, right? Yeah, I'll be there. I never miss the open house. New year, new freshmen." He waggles his eyebrows, and I burst out laughing.

"Good point," I say as we hit the corner where it quickly becomes clear we're going in different directions. "I'll see you in Studio tomorrow?"

"See you then, lovely." He pecks my cheek and takes off for the dining hall, and I turn toward Wilson Hall. If anyone can turn "Carnival Face Painter" into something professional-sounding, it's Caitlin Johannssen.

• • •

Cait looks exhausted when she opens her door. "Lemme guess," I say, strolling inside past her. "Practices are running you ragged now that the boy keeps you up too late?"

"I'm not dignifying that with a response, Francesca."

"So, yes."

"Shut up." She closes the door and lopes back to her bed, collapsing onto it. "Go sit at my desk like the professional we're going to try to turn you into right now. I just need, like, one more minute of rest."

"Take your time," I tell her, wandering over to Samara's side of the room. It's such a funny contrast to Cait's, all floral sheets and pictures of landscapes opposite Cait's plaid and posters of athletes. There aren't many personal photographs on Samara's side either, but I pick up one of the two framed on her nightstand and look at it closely, recognizing Cait's roommate between the two other girls in the frame.

Yup, still gorgeous.

"Are you going through Sam's stuff?" Cait asks without so much as looking in my direction.

"What are pictures for if not to be looked at?"

"Don't touch her stuff, Frankie."

"All right, all right." I bend to sniff the perfume bottle on her desk without using my hands. It smells like sunshine and orange blossoms, and makes my mouth water.

"You're being creepy."

"Shut up and rest." I move on to her bookshelf, which is full of pretty standard textbooks, and then a whole bunch of colorful spines with names of books I don't recognize. I don't think they're romance novels, but...young adult, maybe? And then there's a lone skinny volume in a language I can neither read nor identify. "Any idea what language this is? It's gorgeous. The letters look kinda like runes."

"Well, she's part Armenian, so...I'm guessing Armenian."

"Cool."

"Okay, seriously, get out of her stuff and go sit your ass down at my desk." I hear a shuffling, and Cait's off her bed and in full drill sergeant mode. "So what are we adding to this thing?"

I run down whatever I can think of for Cait, who turns "Carnival Face Painter" into "Childcare Specialist with Focus on Fine Arts" and paints my mandated three hours a week of bible study with my father as some sort of internship in religious studies. I'm not entirely sure what I look more qualified for now than I did half an hour ago, but I sure sound fancier.

"You are brilliant," I tell her with a smacking kiss on her cheek as she prints out two copies on stiff, fancy paper. "You are going to be the best lacrosse-playing finance person with a passel of crazily tall, beautiful brown babies in the universe."

She rolls her eyes. "I already fixed your resume, Frankie. The time to suck up is *before* I do you the favor."

"Isn't it better you see my love is genuine?"

"Absolutely. Now move your ass out of my desk chair; I have Econ homework."

"Fine, fine. Can I linger until your hot roommate gets back, at least?"

"Oh my God, no. Get out."

I let her shove me toward the door, but before I leave, I say, "Seriously, Cait, thanks for your help."

"Anytime, Frankie B." She pats my cheek. "Don't forget to call the CSC and make an actual appointment. My friend Tish says it can be a total mad house."

"Duly noted. I'm gonna drop this stuff off and head to my Gender Studies class but dinner tonight? Or will you be too busy swallowing—"

"*Out.*"

• • •

The Career Services Center is bustling when I show up at four, and I silently bless Cait for convincing me to make an actual appointment. I take a seat and pull out my sketchpad, idly doodling disembodied lips and eyes until an impatient voice calls my name, brutally butchering both Francesca and Bellisario.

"Office on the left," the receptionist snaps when I stand up. I let myself through the door with "Alicia Wallace" on the nameplate and take a seat across from a pleasant-looking woman with a head of springy curls held back by a scarf and a colorful dress in a clashing print. I like her immediately.

"You must be Francesca," she says warmly, extending a hand.

"Frankie." We shake, and then she opens up the folder in front of her.

"So, you're looking for a job in…" She frowns slightly at my records. "Something artistic, I'm guessing."

"That'd be nice, sure."

Her frown settles into a sympathetic smile. "I'm afraid the couple of internships we had—and I do literally mean couple—both went to seniors. And you're looking for something that pays, yes?"

"Definitely, yes. Please."

She turns to her computer. "We do have a number of work study positions on campus, but many of them require you to be enrolled in a relevant major, such as one of the sciences. Since there are no paid positions with the art department, and your work experience is rather limited, I think your best bet would be a receptionist or office assistant position. How does that sound?"

Like the 13th circle of hell. "Works for me."

"Great!" Her shoulders relax, just a bit, and I realize she was expecting much more resistance. Granted, I guess my blue-streaked hair, multi-pierced ears, and tattoos don't scream Office Drone, but money is money and I'm not exactly swimming in it right now. "Let's see what departments are looking. How many hours a week were you thinking?"

"Twelve to fifteen would be ideal. I need money, but I also need to be able to spend time in the studio."

"Well, that takes a couple of these out," she murmurs, her long, pearlescent nails clacking on the keyboard. "The Classics Department needs a filing assistant, though that's only ten." It's also *classics.* Classic movies? Okay. Classic Greek literature? Not so much my thing. She glances at me, and I'm guessing my internal monologue is plain on my face. "That one doesn't seem to be piquing your interest. How about the Physics Department? They're looking for a receptionist from noon to three, Monday through Friday."

"Can't," I say apologetically. "That conflicts with my Tuesday-Thursday gender studies lecture *and* my Wednesday seminar on Modernist depictions of the female form."

She goes back to my folder and flips through the papers until she comes up with a copy of my schedule. "Ah, yes, I see. Okay. Well, the only department I see looking for a receptionist for morning hours is Psychology—eight to noon, Monday, Wednesday, and Friday. Does that work?"

The idea of getting up that early three days a week, including Friday, physically pains me. But the schedule works with mine, and when Ms. Wallace tells me the pay, that does too. Plus, the Psychology department is one of the closest few to my apartment; Classics is all the way across campus.

"Guess I'm applying for that one," I say, stifling a yawn at the thought. Or maybe I just need more coffee.

"Great!" She gives me the information and sends me on my way, back to my apartment to fill out an application.

But first—so much more coffee.

chapter three

The hiring process is thankfully a quick one, and when we open the doors to our little shindig on Friday night, we're officially celebrating my new job, too. "Congrats, Frank," Cait says as she strolls in with Mase behind her and leaves a huge smooch on my cheek. "You're gonna kick ass at...whatever an office assistant for a random college department does."

"Why thank you, darling," I say, accepting a peck from Mase too, though he has to bend down much farther; I barely reach his broad shoulders. "I think I'm gonna rock it as well. If anyone can...do random stuff with files, I can."

Mase nods firmly. "Good attitude." He offers his fist for a pound and I grin as our knuckles bounce off each other.

"So where's the other blonde?" I ask, peeking behind Cait. "I thought you were excited to bring Samara along."

"I tried," Cait says with a sigh, "but she said she had too much work to do, and maybe she'd stop by later. I wouldn't hold my breath, though."

"The semester just started!"

"I'm pretty sure she was just really sucked into the book she was reading. I'm telling you, Frankie, do not bother. For eight billion reasons, Samara is not the girl for you."

"Well then she shouldn't look like that," I say grumpily, but I accept the point. I lead them further inside, where Lizzie is mixing drinks while Connor gently points out it doesn't really count as a mix when she's filling them with ninety percent vodka.

"Parties are more fun when people get drunker faster," she explains. "God, didn't you learn anything in grad school?"

"Would you believe they wasted all that time teaching us history?"

"Ugh, that sounds so boring."

"You guys are really inspiring, you know that?" I grab a cup and take a sip, which I promptly choke on.

"That's what you get for mocking," Lizzie says sweetly. Connor just shakes his head.

"Lemme guess." Cait's hand snakes around from behind me and plucks the cup from my fingers.

"Lizzie's hundred-proof special." She sniffs it and her eyes go wide. "Jesus Christ."

"Pretty sure that's not on the 'aspiring captain' menu," says Mase, and Cait mock-gags as she hands it back to me.

A couple of girls walk over just then, and hearing one of them call our amateur bartender *Elizabeta*, I can only assume they're friends from her Russian class. I take a sip of my drink, blinking against the potency, and leave her to them, scanning the room for someone who might be up for a little fun tonight. "Mase, any of your hot basketball friends coming tonight?"

"You didn't seem too crazy about the one I brought the other night," he points out. "Judging by the company you ditched him for, maybe it's Cait's teammates you should be asking about."

"Off limits!" Cait declares, digging her nails into his arm. "Especially once she's got one of those drinks in her."

"Everyone's off limits to me, Mase. Haven't you heard?"

"Oh please, drama queen." Cait rolls her eyes. "My teammates and my roommate are not too much to ask, especially considering there aren't any gender barriers to your options."

I stick out my tongue. "You know that doesn't mean I find literally everyone on the planet fuckable, right? It's not my fault you happen to surround yourself with people I do."

"What can I say?" She hooks an arm around Mase's neck and pulls him down for a kiss. "I've got fabulous taste."

For a brief moment, I envy my friends for knowing without a doubt their nights will have happy endings. I didn't invite Racquel—she's strictly a hookup buddy—or my most consistent on-campus friend-with-benefits, Doug Leach, who definitely would've taken the invitation as an opening for something more official. They were both probably the right moves, but the realization I might have zero prospects at a party in my honor is a little depressing. But I shake that off quickly, because I'll happily pay the price of a few Friday nights alone if it means I've got my freedom.

I love my fellow musketeers, but I do not get their whole monogamy thing.

"I thought couples are supposed to wait until they're married to be unbearably smug," I mutter at Cait and Mase.

Her snarky response drowns in the sound of banging on the door, which turns out to be a combination of a couple of her aforementioned teammates (though neither of the ones I've hooked up with, thankfully—that got ugly), Abe, and our friend Sidra. "Hey, lovers!" I exchange cheek kisses with them both. "You made it!"

"Despite your terrible directions," Sid teases.

I stick out my tongue. "Where's Jen?"

"Dealing with roommate issues." She waves her hand dismissively. "She always manages to find new drama. I think I'm over it."

"You stayed together all summer and now you're giving up a week into the semester?"

"Oh, don't even get me started on the summer." Sid rolls her eyes and steers us to the drinks, where Abe helps himself to a Lizzie Special and I pour Sid some juice. "My parents are finally, finally getting somewhere decent on the whole bisexual thing, and we had all these good talks this summer about how I'm not forsaking Islam or the hijab. Then, after weeks of progress, she undoes it all with a bunch of ridiculous phone calls to their house. Like, she couldn't reach me for *two hours* because my phone was off while I was at a movie with my cousin, and bam. Who does that?"

Abe throws back his head and laughs. "Yes, fuck, remember that guy who was in Studio with us for a like a day last semester before dropping? We hooked up that first weekend and he called me every damn day after that for weeks."

"Ugh, clingers." I take another sip of my drink and pull some grapes from the not-so-impressive fruit platter Lizzie and I put together earlier. "And relationships. Why. I can't even imagine how boring my summer would've been if I were tethered to someone here. Western Mass is boring enough. At least Mike helped make it vaguely interesting. And Rowan. And Shea. And Lena."

"You know, you're suddenly making Jen seem so much more bearable," says Sid, laughing. "I don't think I could handle your social calendar. One person at a time is intense enough." Then I see her gaze shift, and realize she's noticed Cait's lacrosse teammates.

"You were saying?"

Abe laughs as Sid blushes pinker than her headscarf, and we talk and drink for a while as friends and neighbors drift in and out. At some point, Lizzie puts on music, and I dance until my feet hurt and all the vodka has gone straight to my brain. When Abe asks if I wanna keep him company while he goes out on the patio for a cigarette, I eagerly join for the chance at some fresh air. But it's chillier outside than I anticipate, and I'm only wearing a tank top with my jeans. After a couple of minutes, I step back inside, and immediately spot a familiar blond head.

I curse the fact that I smell like smoke—something I suspect Samara wouldn't care for—then remind myself it doesn't matter, because Cait plays lacrosse and can crush me with one hand. "Hi, Sam." I give her a peck on the cheek hello, and am rewarded with a nose full of sweet citrus. "Glad you finally put the book down long enough to join us."

She smiles shyly and tucks a strand of hair behind her ear, her cheeks flushing rose. Jesus, she is so fucking pretty. "Cait sold me out, huh?"

"Hasn't living with her for a whole semester taught you she's never to be trusted?"

"I'm Samara, not Andi," she says dryly, then claps a hand over her mouth. "I can't believe I just said that."

I burst out laughing. Andi was Cait's roommate last semester, and Mase's girlfriend...at least until he realized his feelings for Cait—his ex-girlfriend from summer sports camp—had never really gone away. "Wow. Samara Kazarian, talking shit. That was unexpected."

She blushes harder. It's pretty great.

"Come on," I say, linking an arm through hers. "Let's get you a drink before your face burns any hotter."

I cast a glance at Cait as we pass her to see if she's glaring at me for flirting innocently with her roommate.

Yup.

I stick my tongue out at her. "I'm being good," I mouth before offering Sam a Lizzie Special.

"I'm not really a drinker." She eyes the mixers—one bottle each of orange and cranberry juice, both of which are down to their dregs. "I'll just fill a cup in the sink."

I dash ahead to do it for her—I'm nothing if not chivalrous—and brandish it like I'm serving Dom

Perignon. Apparently, this girl turns me into a massive dork, but the smile she flashes me as she takes it in her perfectly manicured hand makes it so worth it. "Thanks," she says before taking a sip.

"Well, I heard you've been working really hard, so."

She laughs. "It's a really good book! Though it actually kind of destroyed me—it's about a school shooting, told in real time from all these different perspectives, and honestly I probably would've just stayed in tonight, but after I finished, I felt like I needed to be around living, breathing people for an hour."

I'm tempted to offer her a hug or...anything else she might need, but Cait is giving me a death glare. "Jeez," I say instead. "That's bleak. Not sure I could handle reading that."

"There are lesbians."

"What's it called again?"

She laughed. "Cait's right; you *are* predictable."

I don't know whether to hug or throw a drink at Cait for talking about me in the room; I'm guessing she's not exactly writing up the ideal dating profile for me. "In a good way, I assume."

"Is there any other way?"

Okay, she's flirting with me. She *has* to be. But before I can think of a clever response, Abe calls, "Franklin! Come here a sec."

I peek around Samara to see that Abe's standing with Sid, Lizzie, and Cait, and this cannot be good. "This feels like something at my expense," I say with narrowed eyes.

"Just a harmless game of Never Has Frankie Ever," says Lizzie, lifting up a shot glass of I'm not sure what. "We need you to settle something."

"Never Has Frankie Ever?" Samara asks.

I groan inwardly. Of course they'd have to do this now, when I'm talking to the most pristine princess on the planet. "It's nothing. It's a stupid game they play."

"It's like 'Never Have I Ever,'" Cait explains, since apparently my mumbled response to Samara wasn't a strong enough clue that I don't want her yelling this over the entire party. "Only we have to come up with stuff Frankie hasn't done."

"And if we're wrong, and she *has* done it, then the person who said it has to drink," Abe finishes. "I'm Abe, by the way."

"Samara." She shoots me a smirk and walks over to the rest of them, giving me no choice but to trudge along behind her. "So, what've I missed so far?"

"Well, Lizzie is correct that never has Frankie ever gotten a tattoo on the inside of her lip," says Cait, "but incorrect that Frankie has never ridden her Vespa into a parked car."

"And Sid here was sorely mistaken to assume Frankie joined the mile-high club with a flight

25

attendant," adds Abe, "but we only made her drink half a cup because she *has* made out with one."

"Plus, I'm just drinking water, so no one really cares," Sid adds, wagging her plastic cup. "Hi, I'm Sidra."

"Another non-drinker," Samara says with a hint of relief in her voice. "Excellent. I can get behind that."

"So you're in?" asks Cait. "Hey, Mase, get Samara a cup of water, will you?"

"Guys, this is not normal. Go play Seven Minutes in Heaven like normal people."

"No way," says Samara. "I still have so much to learn!"

"Including the answer to our question," Lizzie breaks in. "Cait insists you were serious about getting a certain piercing over the summer, while I maintain you were kidding. So, which is it?"

Next to me, Samara's cheeks turn pink, and I have to bite my lips hard to keep from smiling. "Only one way to find out," I say, plucking Lizzie's artfully painted shot glass from her hand and tossing it back.

If possible, Sam's cheeks get even redder.

I wonder how far down her body that blush goes.

Cait coughs, and I guess I've been caught staring at the neckline of Sam's lilac sweater. Whoops. "Really, it's not too late to switch games," I suggest. "Perk of being in college—we don't need to use a closet for Seven Minutes; my bedroom's right there."

"Or perhaps it's time for us to finally toast the host of honor," says Lizzie. She takes the shot glass back—one of a set she bought in the Philippines last summer when meeting her grandparents for the first time—and dings it with Abe's beer bottle until the entire room turns to look at us. "Hey, everyone! You were invited here for a reason!"

"Free booze?" someone calls from the crowd.

"That too," Cait says with a grin. "But we're here to celebrate our little Frankie growing up and getting a job *and* a solo exhibit at an art show during Parents' Weekend." She lifts her own beer. "To Frankie!"

The room choruses "To Frankie!" even though I've barely met some of them, and now it's my turn to blush. Especially when Samara turns to me and says, "I didn't know about the exhibit. That's fantastic! Congratulations."

"Thanks," I murmur, wishing I could sink into the floor. "It's really not a big deal."

"It sounds like a big deal. I'd love to see it. Are your parents coming that weekend?"

"That's the plan." I'm actually pretty excited. Each one of the series I'm having displayed is inspired by one of them, and though my dad's already seen plenty of pictures of last semester's work—a set of biblically inspired paintings—I know he's looking forward to seeing them in person. As for my mom...that's a little more nerve-racking, since I've woven in some of her anxiety and depression, but she's always been open about that stuff, and we're close enough that I know she'll appreciate it. "Yours?"

She purses her lips just long enough for me to remember that she and her parents aren't really on the best terms. "Nope. Mayor Kazarian needs to remain with his constituents that weekend. Something something fund-raising something."

When she tosses back her water for a long drink, I could swear she wishes it were something stronger.

"Mayor. God, that's still so funny to me. So are you, like, first daughter of your town?"

"First Daughter of Meridian. Has a ring to it, I suppose." Even with the smile playing at her lips, though, there's a sadness in her eyes that makes me wish Cait had never mentioned Parents' Weekend. They'll all be solo that weekend for different reasons, but it isn't nearly as sore a subject for Cait as it is for Lizzie or, apparently, Samara.

Which of course makes me feel the need to offer her a distraction. "Well, as long as you'll be on your own that weekend, if you wanna come check out the exhibit, it's open to everyone. I don't know if it's your kind of thing, but—"

"It sounds great," she says, and fuuuuuck, her smile. She has this one slightly crooked incisor, the tiniest rebellion against her perfection, and it fucking melts me. "I'll definitely be there."

Even though I made the offer, the idea of her coming to check out my stuff makes me want to crawl out of my skin. But I just say, "Cool." Cait's walking over, anyway, undoubtedly to break up whatever flirting I might be doing. And for once, I let her save me from myself.

Truly, I cannot be trusted.

chapter four

I spend the rest of the weekend sleeping off the party and lazing around with Lizzie, but come Monday morning, I have no choice but to haul myself out of bed bright and early for my first day on the job. I get shown around for all of five minutes before I'm told there are boxes of files I need to alphabetize under the desk, and I get to work on it immediately, glad that it's an easy enough menial task.

I'm not sure how long I've been at it when I hear, "Frankie?"

I pop up from under the desk and promptly hit my head. "Oh, fuck!" I clap my hand over the injury and look up, just as Samara gasps.

"Oh no! I'm sorry!"

Something about the sight of a beautiful blonde in a jean miniskirt makes my head throb a whole lot less. I wave a hand dismissively and climb up into the chair, ignoring the pain in my skull. "Hey, Sam. Catching me at my finest."

She laughs, then covers her mouth like she feels sorry about it, which makes me grin. "I'm so sorry—I didn't mean to sneak up on you."

"No worries. What brings you to the building?"

"Behavioral Psych. It was already full by the time I transferred last semester, so now it's basically me and a billion freshmen, Mondays and Wednesdays at nine. I didn't realize this is where you got a job."

"Yep, brand spanking new," I say with a smile, glad to see it has at least one perk. "Apparently it comes with some unforeseen occupational hazards."

She opens her mouth to respond, but I hold up a hand before she can apologize again. "I'm just kidding. I'm fine, I swear. Just not used to the early hour. Slow reflexes."

Her lips twitch. "Let me guess—nothing before noon on your academic schedule?"

"Not where I can help it. But you look like a morning person." She really does. Her golden skin glows, there's not a single blond hair out of place in her ponytail, and even her manicure's pristine. She's exactly the kind of put-together that screams high-maintenance. It isn't my type, but it's certainly nice to look at. "Are you?"

"Something like that." She pauses to sip from the cup in her hand, and I watch with envy, for both the coffee I was running too late to grab and the cup itself for touching that perfect pink mouth. "Maybe you can make it an early night, especially after that party."

"That party was just the beginning," I say with a wink, sinking into my new desk chair. "It's Rainbow House Welcome Night, and a bunch of us usually go to XO after."

Samara blinks like I've just spoken in Chinese, which, sadly, I can't do beyond whatever swears my friend Lili's taught me. Huh. Maybe she really is straight. "Rainbow House is the LGBTQIA group on campus. Seems to make new kids happy to see out-and-proud old-timers there, so Abe and I always make sure to go. Anyone's welcome."

Samara nods slowly, still looking at a bit of a loss, and I have to remind myself she's from the south; who knows if she's ever met another openly queer person in her life? "And XO?"

"Gay club. It's fun." I smile slowly as an idea forms in my brain. "You should come tonight."

"Me? Come to, um, to…that?" God, she can't even say it. She doesn't look horrified, or offended; I'm not really sure *what* she's feeling. Finally, she says, "I don't think that's really my thing, but thank you." I guess she feels bad for shutting it down, though, because then she says, "but the art show y'all were talking about sounds like a lot of fun. That's open to everyone, right?"

"Yup," I confirm, wishing I could get more of a read on her turning down the Rainbow House invite. "Next Friday night at the Swaine Gallery."

"Cool," she says with that agonizingly pretty smile. "That's in town, right? Hopefully I can manage that without getting lost."

"I'll make sure to get you good directions," I offer. "Here." I give her my phone. "Put in your number and I'll text you." If Cait were here, she'd probably smack me upside the head, while Lizzie would laugh at me for being so obvious, but, well, they can suck it.

"Oh, well, even better." She types in her digits as I watch, admiring her long, thin fingers tipped with short pink nails. "Looking forward to it."

The way she says it, it almost sounds like a date. This conversation is so many mixed messages, I'm not sure if I'm dealing with a closet case or just a sweet straight girl who's so clueless she has no idea when a girl's flirting with her. There's certainly no question of *my* being a rainbow poster child, and she's clearly okay with it, but anything beyond that is a total mystery to me. I take my phone back and send her a quick text. "There, now you have me," I say when her phone beeps with my message, which is just a shameless winking emoji. "Hope I live up to expectations."

Is that a blush? I'm pretty sure that's a blush. "I'm sure you will," she says, a little mumbly. "I have to run to my next class. I'll see you...Wednesday at nine, I guess."

I steal her line. "Looking forward to it." And so help me God, I really am.

• • •

Rainbow House is brimming over with people by the time I show up that night. Everyone who enters gets one of those "Hello, My Name Is" stickers, only these say, "Hello, My Pronouns Are." I grab one and a purple Sharpie, scrawl on "She/Her," and search my shirt for a stretch of fabric large enough to hold it. I end up sticking it just above the hem of my glittery halter, then go off in search of familiar faces. I don't spot Abe or Sid right away, but I do accept an excited hug from Emily Strother, who's wearing an "I Heart My Gonads" pin affixed to her sweater.

"Solid accessory choice," I say, flicking it with a grin.

"Oh, I went all out tonight," she says, holding up a hand so I can see her nails, neatly painted yellow with open purple circles in the centers. "Intersex flag, bitchez."

"Nice."

"I like showing off my pride where it's appreciated." She blows on her nails and brushes them along her pin, then flips her long brown hair over her shoulder so that her hot-pink streaks catch the light. "I think I'm gonna skip out on XO, though. Too depressingly low on guys who like girls."

This is where I'd normally talk her into going anyway, but the truth is, I'm not as psyched at the idea of it tonight as I usually am. Introducing a job into my schedule has me more tired than I anticipated. Hopefully, a couple of hours surrounded by My People rather than Psych students will pick me up. Because right now, I just feel like I'm a billion years old and need a nap.

"Did I just hear correctly?" Abe swoops in and wraps an arm around each of us, smacking a kiss on each of our cheeks. "Skipping XO?"

"Unless you've changed your mind and suddenly like boobs," Emily says pointedly.

"You'd probably have better luck if *you* did that," I remind her.

She grins. "Touché."

We continue to chat over our soda cups, occasionally pausing in our conversation to greet obvious newbies. A cute but definitely freshman guy comments on Emily's pin, and while she gives the quick-fire explanation of Complete Androgen Insensitivity Syndrome I've heard from her a few times before, and Abe taps out texts on his phone, I let my gaze travel the room.

It lands on a gorgeous androgynous redhead with alabaster skin, legs up to the ceiling, and a sticker reading "They/Them" in a firm, slanted hand. They're working both of my biggest weaknesses at once—red hair and suspenders—but I just can't seem to get it up. My brain is too occupied by wondering what Samara would've made of Rainbow House if she'd actually come.

Would she have relaxed and hung out? Would she have felt weird or made uncomfortable jokes? She seemed pretty turned-off by the idea of coming tonight, but was that because of us, or because of her?

"You all right there, buddy?" Abe asks, clapping me on the back as if he heard me choking. Then I guess he spots the redhead, because he says, "Ah. You going over there or what? They're eye-fucking you hard enough to burn through your non-existent shirt."

I glance over their way, and Abe is...not wrong. And oh God, are they wearing actual suit pants? My heart is buzzing...

No, wait, that's my cell phone, in the ass pocket of my tightest jeans. I slip it out to read the text, and am jolted by the sight of Samara's name. *Any chance your invite for tonight still stands?*

To say that text was unexpected is an understatement.

The answer is *Fuck yes* but that seems a little overeager. Then again, subtlety doesn't really go with this outfit. As I mentally formulate a slightly more normal response, another text comes in.

I'm sorry, I don't know why I just asked that. I can't. I'm just having a bad night.

There's a twinge in my chest and I can't even pinpoint why, whether it's because she can't come here or because I'm the closest person she had to contact or because I just do not fucking like a girl that sweet being that sad. *You wanna talk about it?*

That's okay, thx. Have fun w/your friends.

I glance at the redhead, who's now chatting with some girl, and then at Abe, who's telling a joke to Sid, Emily, and a cute guy with black hair I'm guessing is his target for the night. Pretty sure no one will miss me if I slip out. *It's cool. I'd rather talk to you if you need it.* I hesitate before my next text, not sure if I'm crossing over into "too pushy" territory, then tell myself she can always say no if I am. *I can come over, if you want.*

Admittedly, I'm pretty surprised when she writes back, *That'd...actually be really nice if you don't mind. I hate to bother you, but I could use a friend.*

I look down at my sparkly halter-top, second-skin jeans, and fuck-me shoes. Not the friendliest attire, but I like that Samara wants to confide in me, that I could maybe make her feel better. Much as I enjoy booty calls, I get those far more frequently than I get ones like this. Of course, I wouldn't have any complaints about Samara wanting me for my booty, but I like that she wants me for my ear.

I like it a lot.

Which feels weird.

No bother, I assure her. *Just gimme 20 minutes.* Enough time to say my goodbyes, jump on my Vespa, and head straight over. *30 if you want me to pick up pizza.* The best way I know to improve a bad night if you don't drink.

I'll take care of the pizza, she writes back, and I'm back to mentally playing "Date or No Date." No, wait, this is obviously *not* a date. (And since when have I ever *wanted* anything to be a date, anyway?) She texted me as a friend, and all we're doing is hanging out and talking. It just happens to be that one of us is obscenely cute, and the other one would like to fuck her six ways from Sunday. No bigs. *Any requests?*

It takes me a second to realize she means regarding the pizza. *Surprise me*, I write back, and then I slip my phone back into my pocket and say my goodbyes.

• • •

I end up needing twenty-five minutes to get to her room, because Abe insists on some quick gossip about the cute dark-haired guy, but for my seldom-punctual ass, that's actually pretty good. In any case, when she answers the door in her usual way-too-flattering yoga wear, I'm pretty sure my five-minute lateness isn't the reason for her red-tinged eyes and nose.

"You've been crying," I say, because I'm too dumb to filter myself. "Shit. Is everything okay?"

"Guess I didn't hide it as well as I thought." She sniffles even as she smiles a little. "Sorry, I'm so gross right now."

"You literally could not be gross if you tried," I say, settling onto Cait's bed.

She laughs weakly. "You should talk. That's quite the outfit."

"I thought I was going to a club tonight," I say sheepishly.

"I know. I'm sorry to drag you out like that."

"Trust me, I was perfectly happy to be dragged out. What hap—"

A buzzing sound cuts me off. "Pizza guy must be downstairs," says Sam, hopping up from her desk chair. "I'll be right back." I try not to stare at her ass when she moves to the door—*friends*—but those fucking yoga pants make it impossible.

I make myself comfortable as the door closes behind her, peeling off my heels and changing into a pair of Cait's shorts; those pants weren't really made for pizza-eating. By the time Samara returns I'm comfortably stretched out on Cait's bed, staring at the cheesy glow-in-the-dark stars on her ceiling.

"Wasn't sure what you'd like," she says. "I was craving barbecue chicken, but I didn't know if you preferred vegetarian, so I got that too. And one pepperoni, just in case."

Her melodious accent is a little thicker than usual, or maybe I've just never heard her say "barbecue" before. Either way, I want her to say it again. "Sounds perfect," I say. "All of them." I'm not just being nice; I really like pizza.

"Good." She puts the box on her desk and opens it up, filling the room with the mouthwatering scents of tangy sauce, spicy meat, and yeasty crust. If she notices I've changed into Cait's shorts, she doesn't acknowledge it, just takes out a couple of paper plates from a cabinet in their kitchenette, puts a slice on each, and hands me one. I move to Cait's desk to eat—there are no other tables in their double—and accept a full glass. "It's sweet tea," she says as I take a sip, and indeed it is. "Y'all have no idea how to make decent iced tea up here."

Her words are joke-y enough, but she looks deflated as she says them, which adds a little more fuel to my suspicions that it's shit from home that's ruined her night. "Thank you for taking the time to right our wrongs," I say in mock-seriousness, putting down the glass. "As a show of gratitude, how about I listen to you tell me what happened tonight?"

She'd been lifting a slice to her lips, but she puts it back down as if my question's made her lose her appetite. "It's not import—"

"Sam. Don't you dare."

She sighs. "My family's just... Well, I told you how it was a huge fight when I said I needed to get out of South Carolina and transfer to college up north, right? And finally my parents agreed *if* I majored in Poli-Sci, kept my GPA above a 3.5, came home for every break, et cetera, et cetera?"

"Vividly." We talked about it last semester, the night we met. Cait had ditched us at a basketball game to talk to Mase, and Samara and I went out to dinner alone. Most of the conversation between us that night was just superficial stuff about Radleigh and what people do for fun around campus—Sam was a new transfer then—but after I watched her send a series of calls to voicemail, the stuff about her parents had come tumbling out.

"Well, they've been adding more conditions, including demanding I drop my creative writing elective so I can pick up a useless American history class *and* choosing some friend's son at Cornell they want me to date. But the worst part is—" She cuts herself off and glances toward Cait's bed, as if she'd somehow materialized there in the last ten minutes.

"Cait's not here," I say softly. "Whatever it is, you can tell me."

Her cheeks flush as she picks at a piece of chicken on her pizza. "They want to pull me out of the dorm, put me in my own apartment."

"Why?"

"My mom saw Mase earlier today when she and I were Skyping and he came to pick up Cait. After they left, she asked me who he was and said she didn't feel safe with me living in a room 'a man like that could walk into whenever he wants.'"

Anger bubbles up in me. "Is she fucking serious? Because he's black?"

She nods miserably. "I mean, she didn't *say* that, of course, but it's not hard to guess. Runs in the family—my mom's parents hated my dad the second they heard the name Kazarian; couldn't get over how ethnic it was. It was only when he met them and proved he looked and sounded as WASP-y as they do that they calmed down. You'd have no idea my dad has any Armenian blood if not for that name. Lord knows he never, ever acknowledges it; I *know* he'd have changed it if his parents wouldn't have disowned him. He's gotta be a Good Ol' Boy for Meridian and all the other South Carolinians he's hoping will vote him into the senate someday. Five generations of Clemson grads. Yet another reason I'm a raging disappointment."

"Sam—"

"Not to mention my chosen reading material," she continues as I haven't spoken, her accent thickening with every rant. "Doesn't matter that I do all my reading for school, that my parents combined probably read five books a year—they have to make sure to tell me how utterly infantile it is that I read 'children's books.' Y'all'd think YA was written by Dr. Seuss. I told them this is why my dad will never get the youth vote. He did not like that very much."

I can't help smiling at that, and after a few moments, so does she. "I recommended a really good political one about a girl whose dad is running for president, but he was not amused. Might've been the hot-pink cover."

Her smile turns impish, and I crack up. "I love your version of being a bad girl," I tell her, shaking my head. "It's so damn fitting."

"So you're saying I'm a dork."

"I'm not saying that," I assure her. "I'm just not...not saying that."

She puts on an offended face that lasts for all of two seconds before she falls apart laughing. I take a bite of pizza and finally, she does too. We eat in silence for a minute and then I ask, "So, what are you gonna do?"

"I have no idea," she says, her shoulders slumping. "I can't afford to be here without my parents paying for everything; I've spent the summers making 'appearances' with my dad instead of getting an actual job. And I don't wanna leave the dorm—I like it here, and I like living with Cait. I don't wanna be by myself, and I don't wanna leave her with a stranger."

"Trust me, I remember that guilt well." I take a sip of the tea, which is growing on me. "When I left her last semester to move into Lizzie's apartment, I felt so shitty about it. But it was a whole lot cheaper, with much better space for me to do my art." Plus, I knew Lizzie didn't exactly have potential roommates lining up at her door, and I couldn't let her live alone right after her brothers left.

Samara sighs. "Is it…is it actually okay if we don't talk about it anymore? I mean, I really appreciate you discussing it with me, but I just feel like I'm gonna explode right now."

"Of course. Do you wanna do something?"

She shrugs so sadly, I just wanna hug her around those smooth shoulders. And maybe bite one.

"How about a movie?" I suggest. "Something that'll take your mind off everything. What do you like?"

She thinks about it for a minute. "*Pitch Perfect* usually works when I'm in a bad mood."

"*Pitch Perfect* it is." I finish my slice while she sets it up on her laptop, and try to figure out where I should sit to watch. Cait's bed is definitely the safer move, but not terribly practical for watching on a small screen. Besides, safe isn't a whole lot of fun. "Okay if I join you?"

"Of course." She pulls the laptop into her bed and I stretch out at her side, inhaling her clean, fresh scent. She's got all these frilly pillows, and her sheets are so girly, it's cute as hell. But I'm here to be a friend, and if

I had any ideas of forgetting that tonight, well, that's what Cait's half of the room is there to remind me.

We watch in pleasant silence, but when the tryout scene comes on, Sam starts humming along to "Since U Been Gone," and I can tell she wants to sing along so badly, she's busting at the seams. "You can sing, you know," I whisper.

She laughs. "Trust me, I can't. Not that high, anyway. And I'm not embarrassing myself in front of you."

I love that she adds "in front of you," as if I'm someone she has to impress. "Oh, come on. Now you *have* to."

"No way!"

"Your loss." Anna Kendrick's character comes onscreen and starts singing "Cups," and I joyfully sing along with her. I have a terrible voice, but thankfully, I was born without the shame gene. Samara cracks up, burying her face in my shoulder.

Totally worth it.

"See? If I can, you can."

She just snorts and says nothing, but…she also doesn't move her head. It's now half resting on my shoulder, and I very happily leave it there. It takes supreme restraint not to touch her any further—to trail my fingertips down her arm or play with the ends of her shiny hair—but I have to admit it: this is nice.

chapter five

I don't have work the next morning, but I wake up bright and early anyway, memories of barbecue chicken pizza and orange-blossom hair sharp in my brain. I pull out my sketchpad, start a pot of coffee going, and curl up on the couch. I get so lost in etching thin but full arches above long-lashed almond-shaped eyes that I don't even notice Lizzie's gotten up too until she's standing over me with a cup of fragrant coffee, asking, "Who's that?"

I drop the pad, then quickly pick it back up and turn it over on the coffee table. "No one. Just doodling." I nod at the "Half Filipino is Better than None" mug in her hand. "Couldn't even bring me some of the coffee I made, huh?"

"Looks like you've been up for a while, so maybe if you weren't so lost in 'no one,' you'd already have your own." She grabs for the sketchpad, turns it over, and laughs. "Oh God. Cait is going to kill you."

"There's nothing to kill me over." I stride past her into the kitchen and pour my own cup. "I draw my friends all the time."

"First thing in the morning. Before coffee. Okay. Let's see all the loving sketches you have of me in this thing, Frankie B."

"Oh, shut up."

A smile spreads across Lizzie's face. "You have a little crush! Oh, Frank, that is so cute."

"I do *not* have a crush."

She bursts out laughing. "You *so* do. You should see your face right now. You *never* get this red, except when someone's complimenting your art. Did something happen?"

"No, nothing happened." Oh, what the hell. "We just hung out last night. Watched a movie. It was no big deal."

"I thought last night was your Rainbow night."

"It was—I went to the house, and then I went to keep Sam company. She was having a tough night."

"And she called you?"

I groan. "Don't make it more than it is."

She settles into the corner of the couch across from where I'd been sitting. "Are you sure that I am?"

I just roll my eyes and sip my coffee. "What are you doing up so early, anyway?"

"I have therapy at ten. I had to rearrange my week because Max and Ty are apparently having a really tough time with the anniversary coming up, and Nancy thinks me going home for a bit would help, so...shit." Her face falls. "Your art show. Frank, I'm so sorry."

My stomach flips a little at the thought of not having half of my biggest support system at Radleigh there, but I can't exactly be upset about my best friend needing to be with her little brothers during a milestone in the mourning of their parents' death. "Oh, please," I say, waving my free hand. "I'll be fine. Your brothers need you."

"Make sure Cait takes a billion pictures for me," she says warmly, then glances at her watch. "Shit, I have to get dressed." She drains the rest of her mug and hops off the couch. "Samara's going, right? On Friday?"

"Yes, Lizzie. Samara is going." Which makes a whole new group of butterflies take place in my stomach, but that's nothing out of the ordinary; I always get anxious about people seeing my art, seeing as it's the most personal I get with anyone outside my inner circle. Intellectually I know a person isn't their work, but emotionally...it can definitely be a challenge to separate the two.

She grins. "Good." Then she closes herself in her room, smug in having gotten in the last word. I would throw my pencil at her door, but the sketching bug is still making my hands twitch. I put down my coffee, pick up my pad and pencil, and get back to work.

• • •

By the time I drag my butt into work on Friday morning, "I'm sorry" has quickly become my least favorite phrase on the planet.

"I'm sorry," my dad said about not being able to come because a friend of his from seminary days had to bail on officiating a wedding thanks to the flu and begged him to step in.

"I'm sorry," my mom said about not being able to come because she has phobias of both driving long distances alone and public transportation.

"I'm sorry," Cait said about having to bail on the art show because of some mandatory athletes' dinner.

"I'm sorry," Sid said about having to spend the night with her parents at the special dinner being thrown by the campus's Muslim community center in honor of Parents' Weekend.

"I'm sorry," Abe said about having to spend the night with *his* parents, who made reservations at a nice restaurant to surprise him.

"I'm sorry," I mutter to my enormous cup of coffee. "I am about to pound the shit out of you while wishing you were full of rum."

"Did you just…?" I look up to see Samara eyeing me quizzically. "Are you talking to your coffee?"

"Not anymore," I say sheepishly, putting it down on the front desk I have to start manning in two minutes. "It's been a rough week."

"Armchair Psychology lunch didn't help?" she teases, referring to Wednesday, when we ate together in the quad when I got off work and she taught me different random diagnoses so we could assign them to total strangers who walked by, complete with imaginary backstories.

I laugh at the memory. "Armchair Psychology lunch *definitely* helped," I assure her. "Just things with the show tonight not going super smoothly."

"Oh no! It's still happening, right?"

"Oh, yeah, I mean, it's nothing with the actual event—just a lot of people bailing." I pick the coffee back up, wrapping my fingers around its soothing warmth. I don't want to unload about my parents not showing up this weekend to someone whose are a nightmare 24/7, so I keep it vague. "These kinds of things make me nervous, so it's hard not having my usual hand-holders."

She smiles softly, and it is not making me melt. It is not it is not it is not. "Well, I'm obviously not Cait or Lizzie, but I'll happily hold your hand." Her face flushes, and oh my fuck yes okay I am definitely melting a little. "I mean...you know what I mean. Not—just—"

"I get it," I say with a wink, though I'd love to see where she would've gone with that if left to her own devices. "And thank you. I appreciate that."

"Least I could do after you turned my night around earlier this week," she says. "I gotta run to class, but I'll see you tonight. Looking forward to it."

"Enjoy class."

"I'll try." She flutterwaves as she disappears into the crowd, and I take my seat at my desk and finally take my first sip of coffee. It's gone lukewarm, but somehow, I don't really give a damn.

• • •

My show doesn't start until eight, but I'm at the gallery at seven thirty, my palms sweating and half my lip gloss on my teeth because I can't stop chewing at it. Otherwise, I look good, I think—Lizzie helped freshen up the streaks in my hair and lent me her mother's gorgeous jade earrings for luck, and I'm wearing my hundred-percent success-rate dress. I just keep thinking about how badly I wish I had a friend's hand to squeeze right now, and I'm not sure the one arriving in half an hour counts, considering where I imagined that hand as part of my pre-show relaxation ritual.

Everyone's been texting encouragement all night, but it isn't the same—not even when my mom sends an adorable picture of my Border Collie, Lump. All I can think about is nerves nerves nerves.

Which I guess I'm not hiding as well as I thought. "Frankie? Are you okay? You ready for them to open the doors in a minute?"

I look up into the warm smile and mismatched attire of Suzanne Kirsch, my Studio professor for the past two years and the one who submitted my stuff for this show in the first place. "Just a little anxious," I admit. I glance at her clutch, which is covered in glittery appliques. "There's no Xanax in there by any chance, is there?"

"Actually, there is," she says with a wink, "but you'll have to choose between that and champagne, so think long and hard about this."

"Fair point." I wipe my palms on my dress and lick my gloss off my teeth. "Everything looks okay, right?"

"It looks fantastic, my dear. As do you." She cocks her head. "Do you have someone special coming tonight?"

"You know I don't have anyone 'special,'" I say, air quotes and all, wondering why it feels like I'm not telling the whole truth. "I—" I break off as the bell over the door tinkles and in (cautiously) steps Samara, looking so heartachingly beautiful a lump actually forms in my throat. Whatever "dressed to the nines" means, she's it, from the tips of her fuck-me heels to her perfectly messy updo. Even if she didn't look infuckingcredible, the fact that she clearly spent time on her appearance for my show is bringing back every weird, stomach-flipping, skin-tingling feeling I have ever had in this girl's presence...times a billion.

She smiles and waves when she sees me, and Suzanne laughs in my ear. "Oh, I don't know—she looks pretty special to me."

I can't even argue. I can barely manage words. And the only thought that fits in my brain is, "Please, please do not turn out to be straight." I barely even notice Suzanne drifting away or the tiny crowd slowly filtering in or the waiters coming out of the back room with their trays; I could not stop staring at Samara's mile-long legs peeking out from the mid-thigh hem of her crocheted emerald-green dress if you paid me.

"Hey, you." She smiles brightly and pecks my cheek. "This is amazing!" She steps away as I'm still recovering from the brush of her lips on my skin and glances around the space. "Is the whole gallery your stuff tonight?"

I unstick my tongue from my palate and force myself to speak human words. "Mine and two other art students from Radleigh. Every year, the department picks three students' work to get displayed in a show here on Parents' Weekend, and my teacher—the woman who was just with me—submitted mine."

She nods, then walks over to the first series, a knot forming in my stomach as I watch the neon light installation play over her glossy golden hair in washes of azure and fuchsia. "I can't believe I finally get to see the work of the famous Francesca Bellisaro." She leans in to examine the panels more closely. "It looks like…scenes from a club?"

"Got it in one," I say with a smile.

She moves to the plaque to read the inscription, and I love watching her face change slowly as she processes the meaning, then glances back at the art itself. "So it's the same party through the eyes and veil of people in different mental and focal states?" she says, stepping back to take in the different scenes. "I imagine the blue light over the gray cast is…depression?"

"Subtlety is a lost art with me," I concede with a grin, and she laughs.

"It's so cool, though." She reaches out to touch it, then thinks better of it. "The blander colors, the way everyone looks just a little more undesirable but daunting than in the colorful but blurry version with the pink light…" The awe in her voice as she keeps examining and interpreting is starting to make me want to curl into myself and hide. Suddenly I wish she'd never come, that I'd just braved this night solo. Because the feelings she's inspiring in me are new and weird and I don't understand why the fuck I'm suddenly sweating under the gallery lights, but I know I wasn't until she started talking. "These are really great, Frankie," she says with a kind of quiet reverence I feel traveling slowly down my spine. "Every time I look at one again, I notice something I didn't before. The liquor bottles reshaped to look like land mines in this one. The women's bodies and outfits in this male gaze-y one. This…it's just so damn cool that you can do this. That you *did* this."

She means it, I think. Lizzie and Cait try to, and they're always proud of me, but I know when they come to see this, they'll talk about how cool the lights are, and which elements of which clubs they recognize. And then they'll stand to the side like proud parents while other people admire my work, maybe staring at it long enough to pick out some details, maybe not.

But I've never had a friend like Samara, who throws herself into things like this, who wants to understand every nuance of what I'm doing, who wants to appreciate art to its fullest—not because it's her life like it is mine and Abe's and Sid's, but just *because*. And the fact that she *does* get it, that she picked up the little piece of my mother in my art that my mom wasn't able to come see for herself…

In a flash, I'm struck with the crazy urge to hold her hand.

I sweep my hair up instead, twisting it into a bun just to keep my hands occupied for a moment.

"You look nice like that," she says with a soft smile. "I don't think I've ever seen your hair up before."

Well, fuck.

I mumble a thanks, then spot a waiter—definitely a grad student trying to earn a few bucks—carrying champagne flutes on a cork-bottom tray. I practically lunge for him, grabbing one in each hand.

"Thanks," says Samara when I offer her one, "but, um, I don't drink."

"Shit. Right. I knew that." What the hell is wrong with me? The waiter's already gone, and I don't know anyone in our immediate vicinity. Nothing to do but stand there, awkwardly holding both.

I take a long sip from the one in my left hand. Then another.

Samara shows no sign of sharing my discomfort or of annoyance that I forgot she doesn't drink; she just goes back to looking at the installation. "So do you have a whole series of these?" she asks. "Do you show a different setting each semester?"

"Nope, that's it. My work from last semester is here." I put down a flute and walk her around the display so she can see the wall covered in my other stuff. "I did a series of paintings bringing biblical women into modern contexts—Delilah working at a hair salon, Deborah as a general in Iraq, et cetera." I stop in front of my personal favorite—Cait posing as Yael from the book of Judges, standing over Lizzie/Sisera with a "tent peg."

Her jaw drops. "Well, that was unexpected. Are you religious?"

"Not really, but my father's a former priest. He thought I should possess at least basic biblical knowledge."

"A former...wow. You have an interesting life, Francesca Bellisario."

I grin, tucking an indigo strand of hair that's escaped from my messy bun behind my ear. "I get that a lot."

"So...your father. Does he have a problem with you being...um..."

"With me being pansexual?" I take another sip of champagne, letting the bubbles dance a little on my tongue. "I think it was a little weird for him at first, but he's had a long time to get used to it. I was nine when I told him I wanted to marry Beyoncé so I could kiss her every day."

She laughs, but there's something so wistful in it, it makes me want to hug her.

It also makes me want to ask, "What about you? When did you suspect? Who was the first girl you wanted to kiss every day?" Because I feel it in my bones that Samara is queer, and every bit as strongly that there is something between us. But I'm the furthest thing from subtle about both my sexuality and my attraction to her, and if she *were* interested, wouldn't she have said something? Made some sort of move? At the very least, wouldn't she touch my arm or lean in closer or...something? She *did* lie on me when we were watching a movie, but I imagine she would've done the same to Cait without a second thought—laptop plus small bed does not equal a lot of options.

My gaydar is almost never wrong; if you're so much as open to the possibility of experimentation, I can tell from miles away. But I can't figure Samara out. Is she holding back for a reason, or am I just completely wrong on this one?

And how do I make myself stop caring?

chapter six

Nothing's made any clearer by the time Samara and I hug goodnight, and it makes me feel even lonelier in Lizzie's absence when I let myself back into my apartment. I can't bug her with my stupid crush while she's home dealing with actual important stuff, and I can't exactly go to Cait about the girl she told me to stay away from. Instead I lie sulkily on the couch with a beer, blast Halsey's *Badlands*, and try to think of anything but those long, tanned legs and how good they'd look draped over my shoulders.

I last about two minutes before I give up, put the bottle down, and slip my hand between my thighs. It takes no time at all to get myself off imagining my fingers are her long, thin, manicured ones, and afterward, I just feel lonelier.

This is fucked up. I do not crush on people. I don't pass on going to clubs where I'll definitely get laid so I

OUT ON GOOD BEHAVIOR

can have pizza with cute straight girls, and I don't rely on my own hand to take care of myself when I'm looking hot as hell and it's plenty early to call up any of my fuckbuddies.

What the hell is going on?

I fall asleep with those miserable thoughts in my head, and when I wake up, I'm determined to make something of my day. Much as I love my lazy Saturdays, if I just lie around here drawing and watching crappy TV, I'm going to go mad. But Lizzie's still in Pomona, Abe and Sid are still with their parents, and Cait...well, Cait's probably around, but I don't trust myself not to blurt out something I shouldn't around her.

Sam's around, my stupid brain delights in reminding me. I promptly ignore it and go take a shower, figuring I'll come up with another idea while I'm in there. Unfortunately, the only idea I get in there is very similar to the one I had on the couch last night.

New plan.

"Doug," I say aloud to no one. I can hang out with Doug. Doug is an excellent buddy, and he is always more than happy to help me scratch this particular itch. I pull out my phone to text him, but then I hesitate. Doug and I may just be friends with benefits, but he's always been pretty clear he'd jump to be more in a heartbeat. I told myself that as long as *I'm* clear, that doesn't matter, but...I think about how confused I am right now about Samara, how deeply it's gotten under my skin that I want more from our encounters than she does. Now that I know how that feels, can I really still do it to someone else?

Fuck.

I scroll through the other names in my phone. There's Emily, but we really only ever hang out at Rainbow House; I don't know that we're really brunch buddies. Ditto a few other classmates who are in my phone for purposes like study group or catching up on missed homework. Oh! Lili could be a brunch buddy, maybe...nope—a quick text to her yields the response that her parents are there for the weekend.

And then there's Racquel. Could I text Racquel? I've certainly booty-texted her in the past. But first thing in the morning seems a little odd for that, and I can't even imagine hanging out with her in any other context; it's just not what we do.

Which brings me back to Samara.

Fuck it. I text Cait. *Hey, wanna brunch?*

It takes her a few minutes to write back. *If you can believe it, my mom actually came in this morning.*

Et tu, Caitlin?

But you can come with us to the PW brunch!

Hard pass. Being at a Radleigh-sponsored Parents' Weekend brunch with a zillion parents who aren't mine is definitely not how I want to spend my Saturday. *Nah, but thanks.*

K, sorry. Xoxo

At this point, it's clear: the universe is pointing me in a single direction. And I can't ignore the universe. I take a deep breath and text Samara. *If you're not bored of me yet, I'm home alone and desperately in need of something to do. You free?*

"Say no," I mutter at my phone. "Please say no."

YES. I've been up for hours and I'm going stir crazy. Have you eaten?

Ugh, she is fucking perfect. *Nope.*

We make plans to meet at Wicked Waffles, which everyone on campus calls Double-Dub, and I take way too long to get dressed. I'd been afraid it would be overrun with Radleigh kids and their parents, but I guess more have gone to the brunch than I'd have thought. The restaurant is half empty when I arrive, making it easy to spot Samara, even though she's tucked in a corner with her nose buried in a book.

She's so engrossed, she doesn't notice me until I'm literally seated across from her, tapping her foot with mine.

And then she jumps in her seat. "Oh my God, I'm sorry. Hi!"

"Good book?" I tease.

"Yeah, it's okay," she says sheepishly.

"Lesbians?" I ask with a waggle of my eyebrows.

She tips her head to the side. "Let's say...sexual orientation unclear. But I have my theories."

"How are you so good at getting me interested in these?" I ask as I watch her tuck away the black hardcover.

"Maybe you're just meant to be a YA reader," she says with a smile.

"For you? I'm willing to give it a shot. *After* I catch up on my art history reading," I amend.

"Deal. I know just the book for you—lesbians right on the cover."

"You're learning my taste so quickly."

She laughs, and I resist the urge to point out that for a straight girl, she sure seems to have encyclopedic knowledge of queer books. Instead, I let the laminated menu hide my smile as I survey my waffle options, and I imagine that she's doing the same.

Once we've both ordered—bacon-cheddar for me and cinnamon-pear for her—I say, "This is on me, by the way. For dragging yourself out to my show last night."

"Are you kidding? If anything, I owe you for salvaging what would've otherwise been a pretty miserable weekend. I love reading, but I wasn't exactly looking forward to three days holed up in solitude while everyone else did the parent thing."

"Considering I ended up parent-less this weekend too, I could say the same," I point out, wanting her to know how much it meant to me to have her there last night. "I would've been completely solo at my own show without you."

"You would not have been *completely* solo. You had plenty of friends show up later."

It's true, I did—Connor hadn't been able to go to Pomona with Lizzie for the weekend, and he tagged along with Cait and Mase once the athletes' dinner was done. Abe and Sid both eventually showed up with parents in tow, and a bunch of people from Rainbow House and art class came throughout the night. For as sparse as it started out, it was actually pretty decently populated by the time the doors closed at eleven.

"Yeah, I guess so," I murmur, wondering how I managed not to let that register until just now.

But I already know the answer. It's because I wasn't lonely for a minute of last night, not even when I only had one guest.

Especially not when I only had one guest.

Fuck.

P.S. You're pushing to pay because you want this to be a date, Lizzie's voice adds out of nowhere, just to rub salt in the gaping wounds of my romantic confusion

Fuuuuuck.

Time for a subject change.

I use the mention of classmates showing up to shift topics, and by the time our waffles are nothing but crumbs, we've talked about classes, mid-terms, Samara's favorite books, my favorite paintings, and the fact that Cait still hasn't learned that a bedroom floor is not a replacement for a hamper. Everything feels back to normal, which is of course when Samara pulls the wound right back open.

"I didn't want to ask at your show, but...is everything okay? With your parents, I mean. When you said people were bailing, I didn't realize that included them."

I drag the tines of my fork through a bit of spilled sugar on the coated wooden tabletop. "Oh. Yeah. Everything's fine. Work thing came up for my dad, and my mom gets anxious about traveling on her own, so."

"Like...anxious anxious?"

Oh, right; Sam's a Psych student. Actual anxiety isn't exactly alien to her. "Yup."

"Ah, I didn't realize. I'm really sorry they missed it. I'm sure they're so proud of you, though. I hope you sent them pictures."

That's it. Jesus. She learns my mother has debilitating anxiety and she actually understands what that means and that's all she has to say about it. How does this girl manage to make me feel so unsettled and so comfortable at the same time? "I texted a few."

My voice is a little weak as I respond through the weird flood of emotions I never expected to experience in a booth at Double-Dub, and she doesn't miss it. "I'm sorry," she says quickly. "I didn't mean to pry or anything. It's none of my business."

"No, it's—you're not prying," I assure her. "I'm just not used to people *getting* the anxiety thing. And I would've explained last night, but I know you're already having a hard time with your parents, and I thought it was better if parents were just kinda…off the table."

She smiles briefly. "If only it were that easy to forget them."

I signal the waitress who'd just cleared our plates and order us both teas—it's not hard to pick up that that's a comfort thing for Sam. "Speaking of which, whatever happened with the whole dorm room thing?"

She exhales sharply. "You don't even want to know."

"That bad?"

"Oh, no, it wasn't. Because I lied," she says flatly. "I told them Cait and Mase broke up. Rather than say, 'y'all are being racist jerks,' I lied. I am so, so sick of being a cowardly liar."

A prickle steals over my skin, and I can't help but wonder what else she's lying about.

But I've got a pretty good idea.

I reach across the table and squeeze her hand, just as a tear snakes down her cheek. "Now *I'm* sorry. I shouldn't have asked that."

"No, no, please—that's definitely not your fault." She uses her free hand to rub the tear into her skin.

"Sorry, I've been an extra-big mess lately. God, this is embarrassing."

"You don't have to be embarrassed in front of me, ever," I say softly but firmly.

She looks down at our hands and withdraws hers, and something inside my stomach sinks like a stone. The waitress of course chooses that moment to bring our teas, but I can't imagine choking anything else down right now. I went too far, and this got weird, and I have no idea what the fuck I am doing with this girl. "Sorry, I—"

"Can we go hang out at your apartment or something?" she interrupts. "I'm sorry, I know we just got these, but maybe we can take them to go. I just need to shut my brain off for a bit. Is that okay?"

Is that okay? That she wants to go back to my apartment? Hell yes, that's okay. She's not asking as if she wants the same things to happen there that I do, but for right now, I'll gladly take not having fucked up this brunch into too-awkward oblivion. "Yeah, for sure." I call the waitress back, and she brings us hot cups so we can transfer our teas for the walk back. I also grab the check over Samara's protests, even though she clearly has the money to spend and I most definitely do not. "You treated for the pizza," I remind her.

That seems to placate her, and after I empty my wallet onto the table, off we go.

The walk home is a silent one, both of us sipping tea and taking in the changing leaves. The cold may be killer in the winter, but autumn always makes me love going to school in upstate New York. All around us, swaths of ochre and carmine are bleeding into the green treetops like flames licking at the branches, and they make such a beautiful backdrop for Samara's honey-colored hair and flushed cheeks that all I want to do when we get back to my apartment is draw her.

Well, not *all* I wanna do, but.

"Have you ever posed for anyone before?" I ask.

"Posed?" She stops and takes a sip of her tea. "Like, for a photograph? Yeah, that's kind of a massive part of being a mayor's daughter, unfortunately."

"I meant for a drawing or painting, but I'm guessing you've done that too."

Her lip curls, and I get the impression it's not a particularly happy memory. "Yup, once when I was little, and then again when I was in high school."

So much for that, I think, but then she says, "I imagine posing for you would be a lot more fun than posing for the official portraitist of Meridian, South Carolina."

I whistle. "You guys have an official portraitist?"

"Of course we do," she says in a gruff man's drawl. "We aren't Neanderthals—or worse, Yankees—Samara Jane."

I crack up laughing. "Is that the mayor of Meridian himself?"

"You bet it is." She cracks a little smile herself, and it warms me up to see her smile when talking about her parents, even if just for a moment. We reach the apartment complex then, and I'm not sure whether I should bring up posing again, but it turns out, I don't have to; she does. "So, was that your way of asking me to pose for you, or were you just curious?"

Does she have any idea how flirty she sounds right now? How badly she's making me want to "pose" her over my desk or on my bed or—no, of course she doesn't. *Rein it in, Bellisario. The girl's been painted by an "official portraitist"; she's not looking to get fucked against a shower wall by an amateur one.* Still, it's not like I can possibly respond to that without a little flirting of my own. Hell, I can barely respond to questions at the dentist's office without a little flirting of my own. "That depends," I say as I let us inside.

"On what?"

"On what you'd say if I was asking you to pose."

"I'd say...let's do it." She drops onto the couch and flashes me that panty-wrecking smile.

One thing's for sure—if she's not flirting, she *is* trying to kill me. And so help me God I can't think of a sweeter way to go.

• • •

"When can I see?" she asks for the millionth time that hour. Or maybe it's been two hours. I'm actually not sure how much time has passed. We're sitting on the patio and I guess it's been getting a little chillier, but I hadn't noticed until just now.

"When I'm finished," I say, the same as I've said the last fifty times, but it's hard not to smile with each one. She sounds so damn excited, and the truth is, I don't even want to show her when I'm done, because I wouldn't be able to stand the thought of letting her down. It's not exactly prize-winning work—just a pastel pencil outline of her face and the trees in the background—but the way she keeps trying to peek, you'd think I had naked pictures of Christina Hendricks clipped to my easel.

"And when will that be?"

"Not yet." I fill in her strong eyebrows, then touch up the shading of the bridge of her nose. "Now finish your story." She'd been telling me about rushing a sorority back at Clemson, and though I couldn't fully focus on her words, the comforting lull of her mellow drawl is the perfect background to some lazy sketching.

We're both interrupted a minute later by the chime of a text message, and I glance over at my phone. It's Racquel, wanting to know if I'll be at XO tonight. I ignore it; she doesn't really care whether I answer or not, and I'm certainly not going to in front of Samara.

Not that I couldn't, of course, but it'd be rude while she's sitting here, posing for me.

"Do you need to answer?" she asks.

"Nope." I keep drawing while she goes back to her story, but after a few minutes, my phone chimes again.

"I'm gonna grab a drink of water while you get that," she says, stretching her arms over her head and revealing a tempting strip of smooth golden skin. She walks inside without waiting for an answer, and I sigh and take my phone, ready to tell Racquel I'm busy. But it's not Racquel; it's Gideon, a med student I used to hook up with occasionally, who lives in the complex next door. He must have the night off, and I'm guessing he must've broken up with his girlfriend recently, too. *Free 2nite?*

"For fuck's sake," I mutter at the screen. "You're going to operate on people; I think you can type the entire word." *Not tonight, no*, I write back.

I see he's typing back, and then, *Just saw u outside.*

It takes me a few seconds to realize he has a view of my patio. *Then you saw me being busy.*

W that girl? She's p hot. I'd be down.

"Oh, fuck off," I mutter at the phone, tossing it aside. I'm so not entertaining that conversation. Not that I'm wholly opposed to threesomes by any stretch, but they're not happening because some straight guy decides girls who like girls are his God-given playthings.

While I wait for Sam to return, I darken the shading along her part, where the medium-brown of what I assume is her natural hair color peeks through the honey blond. Out of the corner of my eye, I see my phone light up again, but I ignore it. Finally, she comes back outside, but instead of re-taking her seat in the chair in front of me, she joins me behind my easel. "Oh my God," she whispers, her voice full of so much reverence, it makes me want to curl up and hide.

"I told you not to look until I was done."

"Frankie, this is…wow. I mean, I know you're talented, but—this is such a weird way to see it." She laughs. "I mean, God, that didn't come out right. Just…this is beautiful," she says quietly. "Really, really beautiful."

"I draw it like I see it," I say casually over the weird pounding thing my heart's doing in my chest.

She doesn't say anything, just reaches out and touches the paper, tracing the line of her mouth. I might have paid a lot of careful attention to that mouth. Hell, I'm still paying a lot of careful attention to that mouth. "Do you really?" that mouth says in a slow, raspy drawl that travels straight between my thighs. Fuck, I am on the last legs of my restraint here, and I swear, if she turns the four inches necessary to look at me, I am going to kiss that damn mouth.

"Hey, Frankie, you don't answer your phone anymore?"

What the actual fuck. Sam blinks as if coming out of a daze, and I know exactly how she feels as I snap my head up to find Gideon walking around the building in our direction. Most of the time I like having a ground floor apartment, but right now I wish I were up on top so I could drop a fucking toaster on his thick skull. "Usually, when someone stops answering, that means something."

"Well, I figured you just got busy," he says with a lazy grin he thinks is far more charming than it is. If I recall correctly, though it *has* been a while, Gideon's maaaybe a seven in the sack, a six in the shower. He gets a few points for giving decent head, but right now, he's losing every single one of them, fast. "Hi," he says, turning that non-existent charm on Samara. "I'm Gideon. I'm in med school." He extends a hand over the low brick wall separating the patio from the outside grounds, and it makes me wish we had bars on it. "And a good friend of Frankie's," he adds with a vomitously loaded wink.

She looks like a deer in headlights, but she's nothing if not polite. "Samara." She doesn't sound particularly impressed by the med school part, or anything else about him.

"Beautiful name for a beautiful girl," he says, lifting her hand to his lips.

I want to shove him away from her, but there's no need; she steps back all on her own. "I...should be going, actually. It was nice to meet you, Gideon."

"Please don't," I say quickly. "Gideon's just saying hi on his way to...something else." I am a fucking terrible ad-libber. "Aren't you, Gid?"

"Well, actually—"

"Dude, take the hint."

"No, really, I have a ton of homework," says Sam, already backing away, and I have no choice but to follow her inside, leaving Gideon out on the grass.

"I'm really sorry about him," I say as soon as the sliding glass door is shut behind me, blocking out whatever whining Gideon's doing on the other side. "I didn't invite him here, I swear."

She laughs, but it sounds so forced, it cuts my insides. "Frankie, it's your apartment; invite whoever you want." She pulls on her jacket and flips her long blond hair over it. "I've totally overstayed anyway. You already got me lunch; you didn't have to do that beautiful drawing, too."

The drawing. Crap. It's still outside, along with maybe Gideon, if he's seriously too dumb to realize he's not getting laid tonight. "Please, posing for that was totally a favor to me. If you want it, I can—"

She waves a hand dismissively. "No, please, you should keep it. I gotta run. It's later than I thought. I'll see you...Monday morning, I guess."

The one-two punch of "Keep your shitty drawing" plus "Don't even think about seeing me tomorrow" stings like a bitch. I don't really know what to say after that, so I just mumble acquiescence and shuttle her out the door.

Thankfully, when I return to the patio to get my phone, Gideon's gone. The picture's still there, and I take it down, not bothering to be careful. When I come back inside, I delete all the noxious messages from Gideon, which leaves me on Racquel's.

XO? is all it says, but right now it feels like a lifeline out of a night that would guarantee nothing but me sitting alone and feeling like shit. I allow myself one more fleeting thought of Samara and how close I came to kissing her, and then I write back, *See you there.*

chapter seven

Neither a night of dancing and making out with Racquel at XO nor a day of homework and studio time could make me forget how shitty I felt seeing Sam walk out of my apartment on Saturday. I know I didn't exactly do anything wrong, but I have a burning need to make things right anyway—one that leads me to get up extra early so I can get her a large green tea in addition to my own hazelnut latte.

The wait for her to show up is slowly killing me, and continuously glancing at the door while organizing mail is landing me some stinging papercuts. Finally, I see her, dressed not-very-Samara-like in jeans and a hoodie, her hands wrapped around a hot cup, a blond braid hanging over each shoulder. She looks so cute in this new look it takes me a beat to realize how dumb it is that I brought her tea; I may sometimes run too late to get my morning caffeine, but she never does.

As she gets closer, I realize she might just walk right by me without saying hi, so it's possible I'm a little overly loud in my determination not to let that happen. "Samara! Hey!"

Smooth, girl. Smooth.

She stops, but not without an obvious glance at her watch. "Hey, Frankie. What's up?"

"I just wanted to say I'm sorry about Saturday, and Gideon being a creep." I push the cup forward. "I see you're already set, but I bought you an apology green tea, just in case."

I see a little of the tension in her face break, and my stupid heart gets a little fluttery. "Thank you," she says softly, putting down the cup in her hands and picking up the tea instead. "Perfect timing—I just tried something new and it was not for me."

Well, that's a potentially loaded statement if I've ever heard one, especially when I toss out her old cup and notice it's nearly empty. "Great."

I wait for her to acknowledge my apology, but all she says is, "I gotta get to class. Thanks again for the tea. That was really sweet."

And then she's gone.

"Guess that's that," I mutter, going back to the mail. There's no good reason her rejection should sting more than these stupid papercuts—we were never A Thing, and I'm not looking to be A Thing with anyone, anyway. The whole *point* of college is to experience new things, which means new people and, on a good night, new positions.

Gideon obviously won't be happening again, and judging by last night, I'm kinda lukewarm on Racquel by now, but the semester just started; there's plenty of time to find some people who want to have the same kind of fun I do. I'm cursing myself now for not getting more information on the genderqueer redhead from Rainbow House, and it's making me think another trip to XO this weekend is absolutely in order, this time with a wingman and an eye open for new possibilities.

I text Abe to make plans, then tuck my phone away and get back to work, forcing my mind off of the blonde sitting in class just ten feet away and onto possible clubbing outfits. I keep it up for over an hour of sorting mail, fielding phone calls, scheduling appointments, and handling invoices, and by the time Samara's class lets out, I've almost forgotten about her completely blowing me off.

And then, suddenly, there she is, standing at my desk and looking a little nervous.

"Do you need to schedule a meeting with a professor?" I ask her, pulling up the departmental calendar on the screen. It's all I can imagine she's here for, since she sure as hell didn't seem interested in talking to me an hour ago.

"Actually, um, I was wondering if you'd wanna go to a, um, thing with me tonight. No pressure," she adds quickly.

Fuck, why is it so hard to control my smile right now? "What kind of thing am I not pressured to come to?"

"Well, it's kind of a concert, but, like, a classical thing. Which is probably not your thing—not that you can't be into classical, obviously, but it's not *my* thing, I mean. It's just that Andi's playing in it—she plays violin—and she asked me to come and I felt like I had to say yes. And, well, obviously I can't ask Cait, but I don't really wanna go myself, so."

If that's her way of asking me on a date, her approach needs a little work, but I've also never seen her this nervous, and it's cute as hell. Of course, she might *actually* just need accompaniment to Andi's concert, and she's certainly correct that she can't bring Cait—pretty sure nothing brings on performance anxiety like seeing the girl your ex basically dumped you for. Especially if you and that girl used to sleep a few feet apart. Either way, this sounds terrible—she's correct that I'm not a classical music fan, and I'm not exactly psyched by the idea of sitting in the audience for Mase's ex. There is no reason in the world for me to say yes to this.

And yet, "Sure, I'll keep you company," rolls off my tongue before I can stop it. "What time is it?"

Her face lights up, and my insides go with it. "Eight, at Schneider Hall. I'll meet you there with our tickets. I gotta run, but I'll see you later." She waves as she leaves and nearly trips over her feet. I have no idea what's going on or why I just said yes or what the fuck this internal glow is, but if this is an honest-to-goodness *crush*, I am going to be really fucking pissed.

• • •

I don't realize I'd thought meeting up would clarify whether or not this is a date until I get to Schneider Hall and feel no clearer on the subject than I had that morning. I didn't wanna hear Lizzie or Abe's teasing, and I *definitely* didn't want to tell Cait where I was going, so my usual voices of reason are absent from this conversation. But none of that matters if *I* don't want it to be a date, right? And I don't. I can't. I'm not ready for everything that means being responsible for, everything it means saying goodbye to. And that doesn't change just because a girl can apparently rock a little black dress like nobody's business.

But it really would help if she'd stop looking so damn beautiful all the time.

"Was I supposed to dress up?" I ask as I join her in the lobby. "I thought this was just a little campus thing."

"You're fine," she says, handing me a ticket. "I just felt like getting a little fancy."

"You're fine" isn't exactly a glowing compliment,

nor does it leave an opening for me to tell her she looks gorgeous. Strike a point for the "Not a date" column. Plus another point for handing me my ticket instead of handing them both over together, maybe? It seems decidedly more friend-like.

Jesus, I am making myself crazy.

"So where does Cait think you are tonight?" I ask as we make our way to the fourth row—far enough to potentially hide our boredom but close enough not to be obvious that we want to be able to.

Andi spots Samara then and smiles, lifting her hand in a little wave. Samara waves back and whispers, "I told her I was going to a concert; I just didn't say whose."

Or who with, I'm willing to bet.

We chat about nothing for a few minutes as the room fills in a little more, then sit back quietly as the concert begins. It's not that bad, truthfully, and Andi's pretty good as far as I can tell. Not that I'm terribly focused on the music. My eyes keep darting to our arms on the rest between us, how close they are to touching but not. It would be so easy to reach out and take her hand, to answer the question once and for all. It's not like it's a big deal—plenty of people are out at Radleigh. Hell, just in this room. Sure, sometimes it comes with its annoying shit, but this is a pretty open-minded, liberal campus; I can't escape the thought that if she really *were* into me, she'd have made a move.

I try to think back to when I was a little baby queer, but the truth is, I can't even remember a time before I knew I wasn't just into guys. Sure, I juggled "Am I gay?" for a while, not because I wasn't attracted to guys but because I didn't know there were a plethora of options between the ends of the Kinsey scale, let alone between "boy" and "girl." I definitely played around with different labels until I decided pansexual felt like the best fit. But thinking I was straight? Not part of my particular past.

Sidra is really the person I should be asking; she came out much more recently and would probably have more insight. But she's also a Relationship Person, and she'd never get why all of this is weirding me out so much.

I don't even really get why this is weirding me out so much.

Honestly, this is ridiculous; I get far too much ass for me to get this worked up about one girl. If she's straight, whatever, and if she's in the closet, that's her prerogative. It's obvious I'm exceptionally attracted to her, and maybe that's mutual and maybe it isn't, but I have expended way too much brainspace on this crush that I should be spending on—

A stocking-covered thigh rubs against mine, and I glance down to see that Samara's crossed her legs, making her dress ride up quite a few inches. It's *also* pressing her leg against mine, and there's no way she doesn't feel that. Instinctively I press back, just a little bit, and wait for her to move.

She doesn't.

Okay then.

I'm not sure how long we sit like that, or at what point our limbs start inching even closer, but at some point during a flute solo, my fingertips brush soft, bare skin, sending a little tremor through my fingers. I let my gaze drop to our arms, and I can see hers is covered in goose bumps, but she doesn't move.

It's not the slightest bit cold in here.

With any other girl, this is where I'd push it—trace lines along the silky inside of her forearm, or drop my hand to massage her knee—but I strongly suspect doing that now would spook Samara, and that's the last thing on earth I wanna do.

So I leave my thigh pressed to hers. I keep my fingertips resting lightly on her arm. And I sit through the longest fucking concert in the history of human existence.

• • •

When it's finally over, Sam walks up to Andi to congratulate her on a job well done while I go out to wait out in the lobby; something tells me Andi wouldn't particularly appreciate Samara's choice of company. I check my phone while I wait, and see I finally have a reply text from Abe from this morning: *Sorry,*

Franklin—date Fri night. Sat?

I have a text from Lizzie, too: *Staying w/C tonight. NO SEX ON THE COUCH WHILE I'M GONE.*

A laugh startles me, and I realize I'm sticking my tongue out at my phone. "Who's that?" Sam asks.

"Just Lizzie being a brat," I say sheepishly, sliding my phone into the back pocket of my jeans. "On the bright side, she's vacating the premises for the night, if you wanna come hang out a little longer. We can rehash the...stringwork, or something." I offer up a flash of a smile. "Sorry, my classical knowledge remains wholly unimpressive."

I expect my sadass flirting to put her at ease, but if anything, she only looks more tense. Even though I'm dying to see just how much more she might like being touched, it would seem that portion of the night has ended. "I can also just walk you back," I tell her. "Don't worry, I'll run as soon as you're safely inside so we don't have to deal with The Wrath of Cait."

She thinks it over for a minute, then says, "Let's go to your place for a bit."

There's nothing flirty or suggestive in her tone, but it leaves me feeling optimistic anyway. A little too optimistic, because I offer my arm and she just smiles wryly and promptly starts walking. As I trudge along quietly beside her, I wish I'd absorbed some Psych knowledge from my time working in the department, because I have absolutely no clue what's going on in this girl's head.

We walk in complete silence the entire way, not a word exchanged between us until she says "Thanks" when I hold open the door to my apartment, followed by "Sure, thanks," when I offer her tea. I pull off my ankle boots and pad into the kitchen, searching through the cabinets. I know we have tea here somewhere… aha! There's a box of peppermint that Cait or Connor must have put away, because it's a couple of inches out of my reach. I jump up, just barely grazing it with my fingertips.

I'm about to try again when I feel a warmth at my shoulders. My breath catches in my throat as Samara's long, slender arm stretches over me, her breasts pressing against my back, her citrus-y hair wafting by my nose, and pulls down the box. Only when it's back at her side do I dare turn around, and there she is, no more than six inches away, her lower lip caught in her teeth. "I'm a little taller," she says with a note of apology in her voice, handing over the tea.

"Samara." God, my voice sounds raw.

She swallows hard but continues holding up the tea box as if I haven't said a word. I take it, and the spark when our fingers touch is so impossible to ignore that she visibly winces.

Fuck this. I put the tea on the counter and take her face in my hands, gently as if I were cradling a china cup. "Samara."

She doesn't say anything, but she doesn't move, either. Her eyes are pleading, and even though this is so stupid for so many reasons, I couldn't restrain myself if I wanted to.

The instant our lips touch, it's like a tidal wave rushing through my veins. Even I have to acknowledge I've never felt anything like this, and I desperately want more, whatever she's willing to give. But apparently that isn't very much, because she pulls away, panting as if she's just run a marathon. "Frankie. I can't."

"Okay," I say immediately, stepping back to give her more room to breathe. "That's okay."

"It's not."

I'm not sure what part we're talking about right now, or what the right thing to say is. She's *not* straight; whether she wants to kiss me or not, I'm damn sure about that now. But she looks about three seconds from falling apart, and I'm not sure if it's kissing *me* or kissing a girl or something else entirely that's throwing her. "Look, I'm sorry if I read you wrong—"

"You didn't." She gulps in a breath of air, and I turn away to pour her a glass of water, giving her a minute to put herself together. "God, I wish you had, but of course you didn't." She accepts the glass I give her, but she doesn't take a drink. Instead, she clutches it so tightly her knuckles whiten around it, and her eyes search my face while her own falls with sadness. "You are so..." Her voice drops to just above a whisper. "I forget everything I'm supposed to be when I'm around you."

Chills. Everywhere. "That doesn't sound so bad."

"That part isn't," she says, her gaze dropping to the floor. "I like you, Frankie. A lot. But I've never been with anyone before. And when I am, I need that someone to be..."

Oh. I see where this is going. "Someone your parents would more likely approve of?" I ask tartly. "Someone without tattoos or piercings or colored hair? Someone with solid career goals? Or is it that I also sleep with boys the problem?"

"That you sleep with *everyone* is the problem," she shoots back, then pales immediately. "No, wait, Frankie, that's *not* what I meant—"

As if I'm going to give her a chance to finish that thought. "I'm so sorry you defiled yourself with such a slut. Don't worry—that glass has been washed since I last put my mouth on it."

"Stop it, Frankie. I didn't use that word and I *don't* think that. That's not what I meant."

"What do you want, Sam? You wanna test out your Sapphic thesis on me? You think I secretly wanna trade in my lace thongs for keys to a U-Haul? I'm not that kind of queer girl. I'm the slut; don't you know? I'm the kind who'll fuck anything that walks because I'm greedy, because I can't make up my mind. I'm not the domestic gold-star lesbian you're looking for."

Samara doesn't shrink back from my tirade. She doesn't even blink. It's infuriating. Her tiger eyes are a little narrowed, maybe, but I'm used to Lizzie's fire, to Cait's ice.

Samara Kazarian is a whole other element.

The silence between us stretches into unbearable, and the ire in me fades out with it. My racing pulse is approaching normal when she finally speaks.

"I'm not looking for anything, Frankie. I never was. I just found you. And I don't want anything that you aren't. I don't care who you've been with. And I think you know exactly who you are and what you want. It's one of the things I like most about you. I don't care if you like girls, guys, both, neither, whatever—I just won't share you with anyone else. Not like that."

A weird icy heat prickles at my skin at her words, and I can't figure out what to make of it. Her honesty is scary and refreshing and hot and confusing and I don't know what to do with it, don't know what she expects from me at all.

"And my sexuality is not a Sapphic thesis," she says, her usually melodious voice dropping so it's low and gravelly, twisting up my insides even more. "I'm gay, if you need to hear me say it. I'm not embarrassed about it. I'm not questioning. I'm not trying to change it about myself, and I don't hate myself for it. I will be out someday.

"But when that day comes, I will lose everything. I will lose my family, I will lose my old friends, and I will lose my financial support. The day I come out is going to wreck me, even as I know it's coming, even though I've prepared for it for years. So I'm the one who's greedy, Frankie, because I won't go through that alone. I won't do it without someone at my side who loves me, who has the potential to make up for what I'm losing. And that won't be a casual thing. It won't be a person who isn't monogamous with me. It's a lot of pressure, I know, and maybe it's unrealistic. Maybe I'm dreaming of some woman I'll never find. And it's lousy luck that the first girl I'm crazy about can't be that partner. But I'm afraid that if I keep spending time with you, I'll never find the person who is, and I need to. I need to start my life."

Fire and ice and an element that is neither snake through my veins and wrap around my throat, my lungs, my heart.

I couldn't respond if I tried.

She slips on her coat and I can't do anything but watch as she slides her long arms through the sleeves, clips her long hair into a twist. Then she closes the gap between us, brushes her lips across mine, and says goodbye in a whisper so quiet I barely hear it, so loud it makes the earth tremble at my feet.

chapter eight

I sleep like crap that night, all the things I should've said and all the things I wish she hadn't turning over in my brain. I believe her when she says she wasn't judging me for sleeping around, but it doesn't matter—she's right; I do. And I fucking enjoy it. Being a queer girl at Catholic school meant a whole lot of skulking in the shadows, especially when I was hesitant to bring anyone home in case my mom was having a bad day. After a decade of that, it's liberating as hell to be somewhere I can do who I want, when I want, where I want.

But...

I forget everything I'm supposed to be when I'm around you. I'd felt those words all over my skin last night, and the more I think about them, the more I think they're every bit as true for me. I've been getting sucked in to quiet nights of pizza and movies and games of "Is she or isn't she" that I swore I left behind in junior high.

Fuck that.

Sleeping late seems to be out of the question, so I dedicate the morning to primping. I add a few more colored streaks to my hair with my pastels, put on as much sparkly eye shadow as I can get away with during the day, and thread as eclectic a collection of earrings as possible through the six holes that line each ear. I pull on a low-cut black top that perfectly displays the matching roses tattooed below my collarbones, skinny red jeans that make my ass look fanfuckingtastic, and my favorite studded ankle boots that add a couple of inches to my curvy legs. Finally, the lip gloss that I've learned from past experience whispers "taste me" louder than any other.

I look *good*.

(The better to fuck "everyone," my dear.)

It might be a little bit much for class, but again—zero possession of the shame gene. It takes all of two seconds before I spot a girl in Gender Studies checking me out. I wink in return, and unlike Samara, she doesn't blush; she just gives me an even more brazen onceover and then looks back down at her notebook, so that I could not be more sure we'll be flirting after class. (Spoiler alert: we do. Her name is Natasha. She'll be at XO on Friday night. What a coincidence—I will too.)

Next up is Studio, during which I have zero thoughts about whether Samara would be impressed by my current painting, whether she'd gaze upon it with the same reverence she did at the show. She's definitely not in my head when I drag Abe, Sidra, and our friend Lili out to Happy Hour for two-for-one margaritas (sans tequila for Sid). And when we go out to a movie afterward, and my elbow brushes Abe's on the armrest, I'm definitely not flashing back to the night at the concert when mine and Samara's did the same.

So with Samara so completely and one hundred percent out of my mind, I definitely do not expect to come home to Lizzie and Cait sitting at the table in my apartment, looking so serious I wonder if they've been sent to tell me I've been expelled. I do not expect "Sit down, Francesca," to come out of Lizzie's mouth. And I do not expect "What happened between you and my roommate?" to come out of Cait's.

"Nothing—"

"Bullshit," says Cait. "You don't really think I don't know how much you two have been hanging out, do you?"

"And please spare us the whole 'we're just friends' thing," says Lizzie. "It's just sad at this point."

"You two sure seem to think you know a lot."

Cait narrows her eyes at me. "Well, I couldn't get her to say a single word last night, and when 'S&M'

came up on her playlist, I'm pretty sure I heard her crying."

A lump forms in my throat at the thought of Samara being that sad, about *me* of all people. Her fucked-up family making her cry? Not cool, but at least it's expected. Me? How the hell did that happen?

Still, there's no way Samara told Cait that I was behind her tears. She would never. "What does have that to do with me?"

"I don't know," Cait admits, "but I suspect you do." She takes a deep breath. "Look, I know she likes you, okay? I hate it, but I know it. I've been watching her crush on you get worse and worse since the day you met, and apparently Lizzie's been seeing the same on your end. If this isn't really about you, then I'm sorry, but…it is, isn't it?"

Since the day we met? Holy shit. I don't even know what to say to that. Cait doesn't exactly have killer instincts when it comes to romance, so if she's been noticing it, that…definitely says something.

Finally, I give up and nod. "Fine. Yes. We've been…getting closer. And there may have been a kiss—that's it."

Lizzie's eyebrows shoot up. "Why's that it?"

"Because she gave me a fucking ultimatum—all in with her, or we're done."

Lizzie and Cait exchange a look. "So?" Cait prompts.

"What do you mean, so?"

Lizzie snorts. "You know you're head over heels for this girl, right? You *are* all in, Francesca, whether you like it or not."

"I am not!"

"Oh, yes you are." Cait folds her arms. "Mase was *at* Andi's concert, you know. He's been trying to stay friends with her, not that she's really interested. He was sitting in the back and he saw the two of you all over each other."

I open my mouth to state that we were *not* all over each other, but Lizzie steamrolls right over me. "You think I haven't seen all your sketches? You think you didn't mention Samara a thousand times when you were telling me about your show? You're every bit as smitten as we are, and you're just too stubborn to admit it."

"When's the last time you even hooked up with anyone else?" Cait asks. "Honestly."

I scrub my hands over my face, thinking of the last time I was at XO and made out with Racquel. Of how different it felt, how conscious I was of the missing spark. How I didn't want to take it any further even though we almost always do. Taking a deep breath, I force out the thoughts that have been plaguing me since Samara dropped her ultimatum—even longer, if I'm being honest with myself.

"Look, my father upended his entire world when he was around my age, because he made a life decision when he was too young to be sure of his path. He thought he knew happiness with the priesthood, only to meet my mom and discover that his truest happiness lay elsewhere. And I've never felt like he regrets that decision—or me—but I know he still misses it all the time. I know he hates that the men he studied and served with aren't part of his life anymore. I just...I don't wanna have to fuck up my world—or hers—to get my happy. I wanna know it when I see it. Until then, I'm having a great time on my way there."

"Are you?" Cait asks, more delicately this time. "Because lately, it seems like all your great times are with my roommate."

"She definitely does seem like your happy," Lizzie agrees. "You can tell I'm serious because I didn't even make a gay pun there."

"Ew, you *are* serious." I look down into the depths of my mug. "You really think I should give this a shot?"

"Say you don't," says Lizzie. "If you went out this weekend, would you even want to be with anyone else? Or would you just be thinking about her?"

I cannot even believe the words—the truth—popping into my brain right now. "I'd sooner stay in and think of her, if you know what I mean. Which is gross. I sound like you two."

"Well, I probably wouldn't have said it with a masturbation reference, but the point still stands," Cait concedes. "Welcome to the life of the enamored. It's cozy over here, and filled with foot rubs!"

"I hate it," I say, and even that is a lie. A foot rub from Samara sounds fucking glorious.

"You're so full of shit." Lizzie grins and throws a pretzel from the bowl on the table at my face. "Get out of here, go tell Samara you were being an idiot, and get the girl."

"It's not that simple."

"As much as it pains me to invite a scenario in which I will definitely start finding your thongs all over my room again, I'm pretty sure it *is* that simple." Cait takes a sip of water. "She likes you, Frank. You like her. She's not your teacher, she's not dating your roommate—or anyone else—and you have no fraught and confusing history. This is the dream."

"But what if I can't?"

"Can't what?" they ask simultaneously.

"Can't...girlfriend? What if I suck at it? What if I drag her out of the closet because we think we have some magical spark and then we crash and burn in a week and I've fucked up her life for nothing?"

I wait for them to say I'm being dumb, that I'm not gonna fuck up, but of course the one time I want them to yell at me, they're both silent. "Wow, no response, huh?"

They look at each other, then back at me. "It's not like we don't have faith in you, Frank," says Cait. "It's just that the 'coming out' stuff is beyond our realm."

"Yeah, we're kind of…"

"Painfully straight?" I fill in for Lizzie.

"Hey, I have made it adamantly clear to Connor that if we're still together for his 30th birthday, I'll gift him a threesome."

"Oh, sorry, I didn't realize," I say dryly. "Hold on a sec while I bestow you with this rainbow crown."

"Don't make me throw another pretzel at you. I hate wasting."

"Just talk to her about it," says Cait. "Tell her what you're afraid of. If Mase and I had done that sooner, we'd have gone through way less hell."

"Tell her I'm afraid I can't commit to one person? Won't that make her feel like shit?"

"Not any more than whatever you said to her last night, judging by how she looked this morning." There's an edge to Cait's voice now, and I realize I'm hitting the limit of her patience. She didn't want me going for her roommate, and I guess this makes a pretty good case for why not.

But I did go for Samara, whether I meant to or not. Because I couldn't stay away. Because I *do* like her. Because I want to at least try. There's a reason I risked Cait's ire in the first place, and that reason is five-foot-seven, reads more books in a week than I do in a year, looks obscenely hot in yoga pants, and takes in the world around her in a way that makes me want to experience something new every single day.

I want her, and I'm sitting here with pretzel salt on my face.

"You look like you're having an epiphany," says Lizzie.

"I might be."

Cait reaches into her bag and hands me her dorm pass. "Go. I'll stay at Mase's tonight. But Frank?"

"Yeah?"

"Honesty. Do it."

I realize this is the closest I'm gonna get to having Cait's blessing, and I don't wanna fuck things up with her any more than I do with Samara. It's now or never, and though that thought chills me, imagining ending this night with her definitely counters with a warming effect.

I wrap my fingers around the pass Cait hands me, feeling the edges cut into my palm, and glance at Lizzie. She gives me a surreptitious thumbs-up, and I can't help smiling. I'm gonna do this. I'm actually gonna do this.

And I have a ten-minute walk to figure out how.

• • •

By the time I reach Wilson Hall, my brain is a swirling mess of thoughts, and I'm desperate to see

Samara's face to settle them. I race up the stairs to the sixth floor, heart pounding against my ribs as I near the door of room 612. I can't remember the last time I felt terror like this, but it's the good kind. The stuck-on-top-of-the-ferris-wheel kind.

I think.

I barely even feel the wood of the door under my knuckles and then she's there, surprise on her face, her long honey hair swept into a high ponytail that drapes over one shoulder. One *bare* shoulder. She's wearing a tank top and yoga pants and oh fuck she's so gorgeous I think I might just combust.

"Frankie? What—"

That's all she gets out before I cup her fine cheekbones in my palms and press my mouth to hers. I don't tease this time, and I don't have to—her lips are soft and warm and every bit as eager as mine. A gentle touch with the tip of my tongue is all it takes for her to open up, and she tastes of honey and lemon and sweetness and home.

The sound of hinges squealing open down the hall makes us jump apart, and she steps aside without a word to let me in, then closes the door behind me.

"So, what was that?" she asks slowly, crossing her arms.

I take a deep breath and meet her gaze head-on. "That was me making sure you're a good enough kisser to make up for the fact that I won't be kissing anyone else."

Those soft, plump lips twitch into a little smirk. "And? How'd I do?"

"I should've done that the second you made that fuckhot speech."

The smirk relaxes into a full-blown smile that melts me into a puddle on the floor. "You should also probably do it again right now."

I can't argue with that, can't do much of anything but close the space between us and taste that sweet mouth again. I reach up and pull the elastic from her hair, inhaling the citrus scent of her shampoo as it drifts around her shoulders, burying my fingers in its softness as we kiss and kiss and kiss some more until we're both breathless and losing our balance. Then we laugh and pull apart, and she fills us both glasses of water from the sink in their kitchenette.

"So, we're doing this," she says, only a hint of question in her voice.

I swallow hard as I accept the drink, forcing myself to keep my eyes on hers. "I really want to try. But...this is new for me, Sam. I really want to be what you deserve, but I need some time to make sure I can be. I can't have you throwing your life into upheaval for me just yet."

She takes a long sip of her water, and the narrowing of her eyes over the glass makes me wonder if she's washing me out of her mouth. "So what does that mean?"

"Just…a month, okay?" I ask, my fingers clenching my own glass as I struggle to maintain my resolve to do what I genuinely think is best for us both, even though everything in me wants to say "fuck this" and kiss that hurt, wary look off her face. "We do this—for real—but no grand coming out. Not for a month."

"So for a month, we're…what? Secret fuckbuddies?"

Oh, how I wish just her saying that word didn't turn me the fuck on. It makes the part I can't believe I'm about to say even harder. "That's the other thing. I don't think we should…" God, what's the right word when you're talking to someone you actually care about? It isn't going to be fucking, our first time, and "making love" is one of the worst phrases in existence.

Ugh, if Samara is the virgin, why do *I* keep bumping up against first-timer questions?

"Have sex?" she supplies, as if I've asked her the question aloud.

As ever, I appreciate her bluntness. "Yes. For a month." I reach for her bare ankle, stroking the soft skin with my thumb. "I want to earn you, Sam," I say softly. "I'm sorry I'm a weak piece of shit, but I swear I'm going to try my hardest not to be."

"Hey." She sets her glass on the floor, takes mine and does the same, then cups my face in her gentle hands. "Don't talk about my quasi-girlfriend like that."

The word fills me with an unexpected thrill that courses through my veins and propels me forward until there's no space left between us, nothing to breathe but each other's exhalations. She falls back on her bed and I cover her, mouth to mouth, breasts aligning with breasts, my hands in perfect position to tease at the skin between her tank top and the pants that mold to her perfect butt like a second skin.

I grip the sheets instead, fighting the urge to take this where I desperately want it to go. Everything for her is new, and I don't want to rush it, don't want to push whatever's happening between us. The thirty days isn't just for her; it's for me, too. I've never been in a relationship like the one this has the promise to be. I want to do this right. I want to deserve her.

And in one month, I guess we'll know if I do.

chapter nine

"How do I look?"

"Great," Lizzie mumbles around the pen she's chewing on.

"You didn't even look up!"

This time, she does, plucking her pen from her teeth and laying it down on the course packet in front of her. "You look great, Frank. You always look great. Like, literally always. It's kind of a dick move, if I'm being honest."

That brings a quick smile to my lips, but it turns back into a critical frown as I eye myself in the full-length mirror on the wall by the bathroom. "It's not too slutty?"

"What the fuck is 'too slutty'? Who even are you right now?" Then a snort-laugh escapes her, and she claps a hand over her mouth. "Holy shit. You're *nervous.*"

"Shut up."

"Francesca Annamaria Bellisario, is this your first real date?"

"Shut *up*!"

"Holy shit! I can't even believe Cait's not here for this. She's gonna be so pissed she missed this for a stupid basketball game." Even as she talks, she's grabbing her phone and frantically texting.

"Oh my God, you are so not helping." I tug at the neckline of my favorite red sweater, wondering if I should wear something less boobtastic. Will this scare Samara off? Does it look like I can only think about boobs? Or is it too boring? Maybe I should be wearing something in a print?

"Frankie, Christ, you look like you're gonna explode. Take a deep breath." I do. "Now twelve more."

I stick out my tongue, then worry I've licked off my lip stain in the process. Then again, if my lip stain *does* survive the night, I'm probably doing something very wrong. I can taste her already, and her soft, full lips...

Yeah, fuck the lip stain.

"Okay, I can do this," I declare, smoothing my palms down the hips of my favorite tight black pleather pants. "I just maybe need a shot first."

"You are not picking up Samara—or driving my car—with liquor on your breath. Go put on those hot studded ankle boots and get your ass out of here."

"Expecting someone?" I tease, as if Connor's not here just about every night she isn't at his grad dorm.

"Not if I don't finish my homework," she says, picking the pen back up and tapping the course packet with it. "Even when he's not my teacher, Connor's a pain in my ass."

"They make lube for that, you know."

"Francesca?"

"Yes?

"Get out."

• • •

I know Cait's at the game with Mase, but as I approach the door of the room she shares with Sam, I can't help feeling like I'm picking up my date for a school dance from her parents' house. Not that I ever went to any of the school dances Immaculate Heart had with St. Joseph's, but my mother always says I have a vivid imagination.

Nearly every other time I've knocked on this door, she's answered in yoga attire. I don't even realize I'm expecting her to be wearing something along those lines until she opens the door and the sight of her in a soft pink lace dress that brings out the natural flush of her cheeks just about knocks me on my ass.

"Hi." She smiles, and it's gorgeous, and a little nervous, and it makes me want to kiss her that much more. She's so girly and sweet, so unlike anyone I've ever been with, and it throws me off my game completely.

"Hey. You look beautiful." I debate rising on my toes to kiss her hello, but her lip gloss is so perfect, I can't bring myself to muss it up. "You ready?"

"Yup. Just need my purse." She turns to her desk to grab a small brown leather clutch, and I let my gaze drift over her long, tan legs as she does.

What the hell am I doing? Why did I wear pleather leggings and my great-rack sweater on a date with a girl who wears sweet pink lace? What am I doing on a date with a girl who wears sweet pink lace at all?

"One last thing," she says. Before I can ask what it is, her mouth is on mine, her tongue teasing me open. I barely have a moment to reciprocate before she pulls back with a brief, gentle tug on my lower lip. "Okay, now I'm ready."

Oh right—that's what.

"That was cruel," I tell her as she locks the door behind us.

"That sweater is crueler." She tosses her keys in her clutch and looks at me. "Ready for our first date?"

"I think so. I might need another kiss to be sure."

"Ha ha." She glances around the hallway to confirm it's empty, then takes my hand, lacing our fingers and bringing them to her lips. I know it's meant as a joke, to shut me up, but as we walk to the elevator with the imprint of her hand still burning in mine, I wonder if she can tell that that's made me tremble more than anything yet.

• • •

Vallarta was Connor's suggestion—a tiny Mexican restaurant about twenty minutes away from campus—and it's a good one, simply by virtue of the fact that it's obviously more popular with his grad student peers than with ours. Neither of us knows anyone in the dimly lit space, and I immediately notice her breathing a little easier when that becomes clear.

Having never been on a real date, I kinda had cinematic visions of how this would go—pulling out her chair, holding hands over the table, feeding each other dainty forkfuls—but judging by the way her eyes keep darting around the room, that wouldn't be terribly welcome. Instead, I just sit across from her as if I were going out to dinner with Cait or Lizzie, and pick up my menu immediately so I won't be tempted to do anything stupid with my hands.

"This place is so pretty," she observes. "You said Connor recommended it?"

"Yup. Apparently Lizzie won't come here because she insists they put cilantro in everything, but he highly recommended the chicken enchiladas."

"Sounds good to me. Everything does, honestly. I love Mexican food. Not something I get a whole lot of at home."

"You really do not miss it there, do you."

She laughs. "That obvious? Don't get me wrong—there are things I love about living in South Carolina."

"Sweet tea?"

"Exactly," she says with a smile. "And shrimp 'n grits. Y'all really do not know how to make decent grits up here."

"On behalf of all northerners, I declare that we are shockingly okay with this shortcoming."

She shakes her head. "You have no idea what you're missing." Her expression grows a little wistful. "And I've got some good friends there, still. My two best, Jenny and Louisa, are both at Clemson. They're not so thrilled with me for leaving. They don't get why I had to get out of there."

Now I do reach across the table to squeeze her hand, but of course our waiter comes over right then, and Samara immediately moves her hand out of my reach and takes a chip from the basket he brings instead. Suddenly, my appetite doesn't feel quite as strong as before, but I take a chip anyway, just because they're there.

"Are you ladies ready to order?"

I haven't even gotten a chance to look at the menu, but Samara answers that she is, so I just say I am too and order Connor's suggested enchiladas. As Sam places her own order, I try to imagine how we look through the waiter's eyes. Can he tell this is a date? Or does he think we're just two friends from bumblefuck who came in for some spicy, cheese-y goodness?

It's pretty clear what Samara wants him to think.

(Which is fine. Thirty days. My idea. *Get it together, Frankie.*)

"Are they mad at you?" I ask when he's gone. "For transferring?"

"They were at first, but I think they're too happy at school to care much anymore. Louisa was abroad for the summer, so I haven't seen her in ages, but Jenny and I are fine." She smiles ruefully. "For now, anyway."

It hits me with a pang that she means "For now, while I'm in the closet." Truth be told, I haven't really stayed in touch with any of my friends from home beyond the occasional social media interaction, but when I'm back there, it's like none of us ever left. I don't have to be anything other than who I am with them, and I hate that for Sam, it isn't the same. "Well, now you have fabulous new friends at Radleigh," I declare. "Trust me, Lizzie and Cait are the best people on the planet."

"Y'all met freshman year, right?"

"Yup—totally random rooming situation. Lizzie and I didn't know anyone here when we came, and Cait knew, like, one senior on the lacrosse team from sports camp. The three of us and Matina got grouped by the housing lottery, and the rest is history."

"Fate's a pretty amazing thing, isn't it?" she says with a soft smile.

"It is. First the housing lottery brings me my best friends, and then it puts you with one of them. Fate—or at least one form of it—has done pretty damn well by me."

Her eyes drop to the tabletop, but I can see her smile widening a little. In the glow of the candlelight, she is literally breathtaking. "You are seriously beautiful, you know that?" I say before I can stop myself.

"Frankie."

"You are. Do you know how hard it's been not saying that to you every damn day? I figure now I'm allowed."

"I guess so," she says, but her voice is so low I can barely hear it. "And you're not too bad yourself."

"Not too bad, huh? Praise of the highest order."

She bends her head shyly, and I feel a little bad for teasing. *She's new at this*, I remind myself. *Really, really new.* "Hush. You know very well you're gorgeous," she mumbles.

Gorgeous. I will take gorgeous. In fact, I get "hot" often; "sexy" too. "Gorgeous" is a pretty rare one for me, and I like it a lot. Especially when it's accompanied by her appreciative gaze, as it is right now. "Is it shooting myself in the foot if I admit I'm surprised I'm your type?" I ask.

She arches one of her perfect full brows. "What did you think my type would be?"

"More conservative, I guess." And I may as well admit the other thing that's been nagging at the corner of my brain since we first kissed. "And more... lesbian."

Her eyes dart around again, but it's a small place; it doesn't take long to confirm no one's listening to our conversation. "Is this about what I said that night? Seriously, I cannot apologize for my word choice enough, Frankie."

"I don't need you to," I assure her. "It's not about that. But it *is* a thing. I mean, I've never actually dated anyone before so I haven't had to deal with it, but the girl who helped my friend Sid realize she was bi wouldn't date her because she's also attracted to guys. Some lesbians care a lot about that sort of thing."

"Well, I promise, I'm not one of them." Her hand starts to move for mine, then she thinks better of it and takes another chip instead. "But...can I ask you about that? The label thing, I mean?"

"Why I ID as pan and not bi, you mean?"

She nods.

"First of all, you can ask me anything, especially if you lay the accent on thick."

She laughs. "Oh please, I barely even have one. My mother was afraid it'd make me sound uneducated, so she worked it out of me."

"Well that is a damn shame, because I think it's sexy as hell. And it's not as barely there as you think, either." I drag a chip through the little bowl of salsa as I watch her squirm. "And pansexual felt like the best fit because I think it's the most fluid. Lots of people think it just means attracted to more than two genders— which I am—but plenty of bisexual people are too. For me, the difference is more about how gender plays into the attraction to someone, whether consciousness of it is actually a factor or those lines kinda blur." I haven't talked about this stuff in a long time, and I have no idea if it sounds weird to her, but there's no judgment on her face; she's just listening and nodding. "I don't care what parts you've got as long as you know how to use 'em," I add with a grin.

She laughs. "If ever I've heard a perfect tagline for you."

The waiter arrives then with our food, and although we don't feed each other, I do pass over a piece of enchilada, and she forks over a fried clam. "This is *so* good," she says after swallowing a bite. "God, I wish I could cook. The only thing I have ever successfully made is choereg—Armenian Easter bread—and that was with my grandmother. She left me her recipe when she died but even if I could find all the ingredients, I'd probably destroy it."

"The only thing I can make is lasagna, but I make *damn* good lasagna. The secret ingredient is extra everything."

"Do I get to try this legendary lasagna someday?"

"That depends. My lasagna doesn't come cheap."

"Oh really. What kind of price are we talking?"

I open my mouth to respond, then realize the waiter is watching us, along with a waitress. Out of the corner of my eye, I watch them whisper at each other, and I suspect they're taking bets on whether we're there as a couple or just friends. Part of me wants to lean across the table to kiss Samara full on her pretty mouth—shock them and end their speculating all in one shot. But a bigger part of me feels a hot, uncomfortable pressure at being analyzed. Ordinarily, the field of fucks I give about other people's opinions of me lies fallow as the Dust Bowl, but now all I can think is whether to their eyes, I look all wrong for the sweet, shy, pristine girl in front of me.

"Hey, Frankie, you okay?"

I blink, tearing my eyes away from the wait staff. "Yeah, sorry." I can't remember what we were talking about, and I feel like an asshole. "How's your food?"

She gives me a puzzled look, and I remember she's already said it was delicious, and she was also definitely expecting a very different response from me.

You win, Imaginarily Judgmental Wait Staff—I *am* a shitty date. "It's great. How's yours?"

"Same." I make a mental note *not* to make our next date at a restaurant; I am not nearly confident enough in my dating abilities for an audience. My tongue feels completely tied right now, and I don't think that's ever happened to me in my entire life.

Thankfully, Samara just smiles as if I'm not halfway to a panic attack, and that little curve of her lips sets me back to right again. "Good." She takes another bite, then puts her fork down. "You said I can ask you anything, right?"

I raise an eyebrow.

"Oh, sorry, I meant—ah kin ask you anythin', raht?"

Her exaggerated accent achieves its intent of making me laugh, but even in faux form, it's still sexy as hell. "Yes'm, I reckon you can."

"Good. Because I have been wondering about your tattoos forever. You have four, right? The quote on your arm, the skyline on your wrist, and, um"—she grazes her chest with her fingertips, just under her collarbone, and I wonder if it's as silky smooth as it looks—"these. The roses."

Judging by her flush, she likes said roses. Duly noted. "Two more," I tell her. "One's on my ankle—a chain with a dangling cross—and the other...you'll have to find for yourself."

That lip bite. Fuck. "Interesting. Do I get a hint?"

I pluck a clam from her plate. "That *was* your hint."

She doesn't respond. She does, however, take an extra-long sip of water.

"What about you? Got any?"

She snorts. "My parents would literally kill me. I wouldn't even dream of it."

"You could always get one somewhere they'd never see," I point out, waggling my eyebrows as I imagine going ink-hunting on Samara's body.

"Parents aside, I could never handle the pain. I'm a baby about that stuff. No piercings outside the one in each ear, either, and I only have those because my mother got them done soon after I was born." She pokes her fork at her food, her eyes fixed on her plate, but makes no move to take another bite. "Kind of a shame, since apparently I find them to be a huge turn-on."

And now I'm squirming in my seat. "Is that so?"

"Trust me," she says, pushing her food around. "Conservative is *not* my type."

"Well...good."

She glances up at me. "As long as we're being honest, I wouldn't have thought it was yours, either."

"It isn't," I admit.

"Oh."

"And yet, you definitely are."

116

"Oh."

I nod. "Oh."

We finish the last bites of our food in companionable silence, boldly letting our feet brush under the table. And yeah, I'll admit it—I kinda hope those waiters see.

• • •

It's not even ten by the time I get home that night, so I'm surprised to hear the TV blaring on the other side of the door. I'm even more surprised when I let myself in and see a full house—Lizzie and Cait taking up the couch, and Connor and Mase sprawled on the floor.

"Frankie!" Lizzie pauses whatever they're watching and sits up. "Is Samara with you?"

"Nope." I grab a bottle of Sam Adams from the six-pack sitting on the table and toe off my ankle boots. "Just dropped her off. I thought you guys were out," I say, gesturing between Cait and Mase with my bottle.

"We are," says Cait. "This is out."

"Figured you guys might want some privacy," Mase adds, "but…guess that wasn't an issue?"

"Was it that bad?" Lizzie asks.

"No, it wasn't bad at all, thank you very much." I pop off the cap with our boudoir legs bottle opener and take a sip, letting my mind wander to the memory of Samara's dark eyes reflecting the candlelight, the sound of her laugh, the sexy blush-colored lace against her skin. I would've gladly stayed in her room for hours, talking and making out, but that didn't seem very…first date-y. "We're just taking it slow." Lizzie raises an eyebrow, prompting me to add, "Something I realize none of you would know anything about."

Cait and Lizzie look at each other and crack up. "Did we seriously just get slut-shamed by *Frankie*?" Cait asks, practically gasping for air.

"Frankie whose freshman year goal was hooking up with someone on every floor of our dorm?" Lizzie asks before dissolving into another fit. Even Connor and Mase are clearly holding back.

I sigh. "Fuck you all."

That sets them all off, and I roll my eyes and pick my way to the couch, dropping between the girls and forcing them to make space for my pleather-covered ass. "What are you guys even watching?" I squint at the screen. "Is this *Hunger Games*?"

"Somehow, it's the only movie we agreed on," says Connor, grabbing a fistful of popcorn from the bowl sitting on the carpet between him and Mase. "The magic of ass-kicking and Jennifer Lawrence."

"And Liam Hemsworth," says Lizzie, holding out a hand. Connor passes her the bowl, and I reach over and help myself to some. "Don't forget Liam Hemsworth."

"So this is what Friday nights become when you're in a monogamous relationship, huh?" I ask, popping a couple of kernels in my mouth.

"Pretty much," says Cait.

"But," says Lizzie, stabbing an index finger into the air, "bear in mind *we're* all getting laid later."

Mase and Connor high-five like thirteen-year-old boys.

I sigh again and take another good, long sip of beer. "Like I said, fuck you all."

Twenty-seven days.

• • •

When I wake up the next morning, my first thought is, *I have a girlfriend.*

Then, *Fuck.*

Then, *How soon can I see her again?*

I groan and close my eyes. Then I reopen one and feel around for my phone. Two texts, which must've come in after I went to bed embarrassingly early compared to my usual Friday nights. It pained me to say goodbye to Samara after a single goodnight kiss, but I promised us to go slow and I'm sticking to it.

The first text is from a number I don't recognize, and says, *Missed you tonight.* I open it, and see that below that, there's an additional, *It's Natasha, by the way.* Natasha? I rack my brain for a minute, then remember the cute, flirty, pierced brunette from my gender studies class. Shit. I skip past that one, and see the next one's from Abe.

Lady, where are you? RHHR is here and I'm p sure they're looking for u. "RHHR" meaning Rainbow House Hot Redhead. Apparently, I missed a very busy night at XO while I was sitting nervously at a restaurant, simultaneously trying to be a good first date while also pretending for everyone around us that it wasn't one.

I think she had a decent time, but I don't even know. Maybe she was just being polite, laughing at my jokes. Maybe trying to affect the whole "just two female friends going out to dinner" thing was too confusing—or made her realize that's all we are to her.

Maybe I should stop being a fucking insecure idiot. Jesus, is this what relationships are?

It is with babygay virgins, a little voice in my head nags back. I pull a pillow over my head to drown it out, scream into fabric, and then toss it back onto the bed.

I need to see her again. Is that normal for dating? I mean, I'm pretty sure Lizzie and Cait see their boyfriends as often as humanly possible, but…is that normal?

I flail out of bed and stalk over to Lizzie's room "Lizzie B.!" I call through the door. "I need help and I need you not to make fun of me for it."

I hear some muttering on the other side, and then footsteps. Heavier ones than Lizzie's. Whoops. Sure enough, it's Connor who opens the door with sleep-tousled hair. "Is this an emergency?" he asks.

"Sort of."

"Would Cait classify this as an emergency?"

"She would not."

He yawns. "Then I'm all you've got. Lizzie's sleeping like a rock and I'm not going to enable the carnage that would ensue if you woke her up."

"Fair."

He closes the door behind him and follows me to the kitchen table. "What's up?"

I go right for it, not wanting to waste Connor's generosity with morning therapy. "How do I ask out my girlfriend?"

Connor rubs his eyes. "What?"

"Like, how often can I suggest plans before it's weird? I mean, I know I did this before we actually started dating, but, like, then I kept finding excuses and...I don't know. Does it still work like that? Because I want to see her, like, a lot, but I don't wanna be weird about it."

He cocks his head. "That...I never really thought about it. We just ask each other if we wanna do something and then we do it."

"But, like, you think of a thing to do. That's part of it."

"Sometimes? Sometimes it's just 'Come over, I'm bored.'" He yawns. "We're at school. There aren't a whole lot of options. Especially since I'm not exactly rolling in it."

Lack of funds is definitely a problem I empathize with, unfortunately. It was easy to split dinner last night under the guise of being there as friends, but even that was a stretch for my wallet. "Yeah, that doesn't help. And options kinda dwindle even further when your relationship is a secret," I mutter. "But I guess I don't need to tell you that."

His mouth twitches. "Cute." Then he yawns again and glances at his watch. "If I'm not getting back to sleep, I'm gonna need some coffee."

Whoops. I jump up and oblige, filling the carafe and getting the machine going. "Sorry. It's Saturday— can't you go back to sleep for the rest of the day? Or do you have TA-ish things to do?"

"Neither. For some reason, I let myself get talked into a personal training session. I'm meeting Mase at the gym at nine."

I shudder. "Fun as that sounds to watch—for so many reasons—I think hell must be the gym before noon."

"Really? I would've thought you'd enjoy that many people in spandex."

"Touché," I say with a grin, my mind immediately drifting back to Samara's gloriously tight ass in yoga pants. And just like that, my mind starts whirring. "Actually, you just gave me an excellent idea, thank you!" I grab a mug from the cabinet and place it in front of him, then dance off back to my door.

"Hey, where are you going?"

"Back to bed!" I call over my shoulder. "Dude, it's Saturday."

• • •

"Now it's my turn to admit being surprised by you," Samara says as I roll up my yoga mat the next afternoon, "I did not picture you being into fitness."

"Is that a comment on my butt?" I ask, frowning as I glance behind me.

She laughs and whacks me on the arm. "Of course not. I just didn't think you were into this stuff—first the run last night, and now yoga... Just not what I'd have expected you wanna do together."

It's not exactly the kind of exercise I dream of us doing, per se, but it does have a few things going for it. For one, it's free at the student center. For another, it's a supremely innocent way to spend time together, and actually forces me to keep my hands to myself. Plus, she actually *does* like this stuff, and I quite enjoy watching her do it. So this way, she stays comfortable, we stay under the radar, and it doesn't feel too date-y for either of us.

Only problem?

I am fucking *dying*. This is maybe the least conducive thing to fooling around ever, and while I'm sure she's perfectly cool with that, my libido is turning into a sentient being that's threatening to burst out of my body like fucking *Alien*.

"So what does one generally do after yoga?" I ask brightly, tucking away the urge to ask if she's feeling extra limber.

"Well, I'm usually in my room, so." She rolls up her yoga mat and slings it over her shoulder, leaving me to wonder what to say to that. I silently return my loaner mat, and then we walk into the hallway to help ourselves to water from the cooler.

She goes first, but rather than drink, she passes the full cup to me. Our fingers brush, and I don't know if it's how long I've gone without getting some or the memory of her body being incredibly bendy in that class, but it sends a prickle of heat all through my body.

Being in her room sounds damn good right about now.

Think date-y, Francesca. What do Cait and Mase do after they exercise or play basketball together? Then I see the cart out front. "Smoothies! Do you want one?"

"Nah, I'm okay," she says. "Truthfully, I should probably get back. I have a ton of work to do."

My stomach sinks. There's a blow-off if I've ever heard one. What am I doing wrong here?

Out loud, I play it light. "Work, huh? What's the book about?"

She smiles. "No, actual homework this time. I still have a hangover from the book I finished yesterday afternoon and I haven't picked up anything since."

"A book hangover? God, that's so cute."

She blushes and ducks her head into her cup to sip at her water, and then we walk toward the exit. "It's a real thing," she insists. "If you haven't gotten drunk on a beautiful book, you haven't lived."

"Would I like this one?"

"I think so, yeah. The writing is gorgeous, and it feels so artistic, I can totally see you loving it. It's magical realism, and it has the most beautiful forbidden love story." As she continues to gush about the book, I realize this is the most animated—maybe the most comfortable—I've seen her all weekend. Is it possible she's more into books than me? Is booksexuality a thing?

This feels like another question for Connor.

Too quickly, we're back at her dorm, and I already know there's no invitation to come up in my future. I can't exactly kiss her goodbye on the street or in the lobby, so I settle for a quick hug/kiss on the cheek combo and turn to go on my way, disappointment settling on my shoulders like an ugly hand-knit afghan.

"Frankie?"

I turn back. "Yeah?"

Whatever she'd been about to say, she decides against it. "I'll see you tomorrow. At the Psych building."

The Psych building. It feels almost poetic, with how jumbled and confused I feel. "Yup, 9:00 a.m. See you then."

This time, when I walk away, I don't look back.

chapter ten

The truth is, I have plenty of my own work to do, including a new commission, so staying home to do it on Sunday night isn't the worst idea. Thankfully, Lizzie stays home with me, doing the same, so for hours, the living room has the pleasant hum of old times—her muttering Russian words off her flashcards and cursing when she gets things wrong, and me scratching at my sketchpad while I murmur-read along in my art history textbook. All we're missing is the clacking of Cait's laptop keys as she fills in some sort of spreadsheet thing and we're back to old times.

At least until a knock sounds at the door.

"I'll get it," says Lizzie before I can get up. "I'm about to throw these flashcards into the oven."

I expect either Cait or Connor, but neither one has the southern drawl that says, "Hey, Lizzie. Is Frankie here?"

"She is," says Lizzie, stepping aside to let Samara in, "and you have perfect timing, because I was just heading out."

"Oh, you don't have to go—"

"Trust me, I do." Lizzie grabs her coat and bag off their hook by the door. "I need sustenance before my low blood sugar leads to a backyard bonfire of study materials. Text me if you want me to pick up anything." And then she's gone, leaving me and Samara alone, the room filling with awkwardness immediately.

"I didn't expect to see you tonight," I say, feeling frozen in place by the sight of her.

"I know." She doesn't take off her jacket, and it strikes me that this is a drive-by breakup. Her hands are jammed into her pockets, and she's rocking on the heels of her flats, looking even more uncomfortable than I do. "I just...I'm trying to be mature about this whole relationship thing—or whatever it is—and I thought I should talk to you in person."

Wow. So this is getting dumped. I have to admit, I do not care for it. I mean, this *was* the whole point—for her to be able to kick me to the curb if I was a sucky girlfriend—but it catches me off guard anyway. Because for the first time in my life, I've actually been trying. And what's worse, I realize as a lump forms in my throat, is that I really fucking wanted this to work.

"Okay," I choke out. "No hard feelings or anything." I offer up the most genuine smile I can, but it's pretty shitty. "You deserve a girl who makes you happy."

"Wait, what? What does that even mean?"

I furrow my eyebrows. "I'm trying to make it easier for you to break up with me."

Her jaw drops. "This isn't on me. If you're not attracted to me—"

I can't help it; I bark out a laugh. "If I'm *what*? Samara, in what bizarre alternate universe am I not attracted to you?"

A fiery blush lights up her cheeks. "You haven't— I mean, I thought that's why you kept planning stuff where you don't have to kiss me."

Now it's my jaw's turn to hit the floor. "Sam, I've been keeping my hands—and my lips—to myself because I thought that's what you'd be most comfortable with. It's actually been kind of hellish."

There are a few beats of silence. "Oh."

"Oh?" I walk up to her and wrap my arms around her neck. "If you wanted to make out, why didn't you just tell me that?"

Her face is really flaming now. Too fucking cute. "I didn't—don't—know how to ask...for that. Oh God." She buries her face in the crook of my neck, and I can't help my gentle laughter as I hold her close.

"Sam?"

"What?" Her voice is muffled by the collar of my T-shirt.

"Do you wanna make out?"

"I really do." Her mouth meets mine, two smiles curving against each other until they fade out into a hungrier, fevered thing. In my mind, I send a thank-you to Lizzie for getting out of the apartment, and then I slowly pull Sam back to the couch until we land on it in a tangled, breathless mess.

"God, I feel so shameless," she says, shedding her jacket and curling around my body. "Please tell me you don't think I'm the world's biggest perv."

"Uh, hi, have we met?"

She laughs. "It's different. You're so…confident about all this stuff. You know what you're doing. I never even kissed a girl before the other night, and in case you couldn't tell, I was terrified."

"Are you still terrified?" I ask, sweeping a lock of honey-blond hair back behind her ear.

"That obvious?"

Instead of answering, I press my mouth to hers again. Her hand curls around the back of my neck and I tease gently at her lips with my tongue until she relaxes enough to let me in. Little by little, her tense body melts into mine, and one kiss blends into another, and she doesn't seem quite so terrified anymore.

"So I was really your first kiss?" I can't resist asking when we finally take a breath.

"Well, no—Stanford Clayton beat you to that. But you were my first kiss that mattered."

"Stanford? I got beat by a guy named Stanford?" I sigh. "No wonder you turned out gay."

She laughs. "I don't think I can blame it on the name, but, yeah. That kiss definitely sealed for me that I did not want to be kissing any more guys."

"How old were you?"

"I'm not telling."

"Why not?"

She noses into the crook of my arm. "Because you'll laugh at me. I was late, okay? You were probably...I don't even know what by the time I got my first kiss."

"I would never laugh at you," I tell her, and I mean it. But I also like the way she's pressed against me right now, her fingers idly playing with the hem of my T-shirt, and I have no plans to dislodge her. "Anyway, I wasn't as early to stuff as you think I was. It wasn't exactly easy to meet guys in an all-girls school, and it definitely wasn't easy to figure out which girls were safe."

"Were you younger than sixteen?"

I drop a kiss into her hair. "Yes, I was younger than sixteen. But sixteen isn't old for a first kiss; that's perfectly normal."

"I know. I was eighteen."

"Oh."

"Not a word."

"I told you, I would never laugh at you! I'm just sorry you waited eighteen years and all you got was a lousy Stanford."

She laughs, her breath ghosting over my skin through the thin cotton of my shirt. "Took just a couple more years and I finally got the right kiss."

And I thought Catholic school had me repressed. "So when did you know?" I ask, remembering how I'd wanted to ask her this weeks ago, that night at the gallery. "I imagine you weren't exactly chasing boys pre-Stanford."

"No, definitely not. I was too busy trying to figure out why I kept getting myself in trouble so that I could spend more time with the guidance counselor." She pauses. "The young, hot, female guidance counselor."

"Ah." An irrational flame of jealousy flickers low in my gut and I tilt her chin up for a kiss, just because I can. "How hot are we talking?"

She pretends to think it over. "On a scale from one to Frankie Bellisario, maybe a four?"

"Good girl." I pull her close and kiss her again, and as we lose ourselves in each other's arms and mouths, I think we might finally have figured out the perfect date.

• • •

For the rest of the week, we stick to my apartment or her room, depending on Lizzie and Cait's schedules.

I learn that Samara has a secret affinity for cooking shows, despite not being able to cook. She learns that I have a secret affinity for having the Florentine skyline tattoo on my wrist traced with her tongue.

It's a good week.

By the end of it, though, I'm feeling desperately antsy. Much as I love making out on the couch—and I do, very much—I'm starting to feel a little like a cave dweller. So at lunch after work on Friday afternoon, when Cait casually mentions a particularly big game of Mase's coming up that night, I say, "That sounds like fun. I'll be there."

Lizzie laughs. "Uh oh."

"What?"

Cait shakes her head. "You have never wanted to come to a game when it didn't mean ogling basketball players. Everything okay with you and Sam?"

"More than okay," I assure them both, ripping off the corner of my panini. "I just need to get out of the house for a night, and going out on actual dates doesn't really seem to be working while we're still in this…test phase."

"Fair enough," says Lizzie, just as her phone lights up with a text. "I'd happily keep you company, but I promised to go to some lecture with Connor tonight. That's him now, reminding me that this is an important one for him and I have to wear underwear this time."

"Boo on all counts." I chew thoughtfully on the bite of mozzarella, tomato, and pesto—nowhere near as good as my nonna would've made it—and turn back to Cait. "It's okay if I invite Samara, right?"

"Of course! I'd be honored to be the third wheel on your billionth non-date."

I raise an eyebrow. "I can't tell if you're being sarcastic."

"Honestly, neither can I."

"That's how the two of you first met, right?" Lizzie asks, massacring the chicken leg on her plate. "Maybe it'll be cute to revisit." She turns to Cait. "And since you were third-wheeling that night too, it'll *really* be like old times!"

"Well, hopefully without me and Mase getting into a blowout fight at the end," Cait says wryly.

"I'll pull for the spanking to be less verbal, more literal this time," I promise as I tap out a text to Samara about the game. Immediately, I can see her typing back, but for some reason, it takes almost a full two minutes before she sends, *Sure.* Then another thirty seconds for, *Sounds fun.*

"We'll be there," I tell Cait, hoping Sam's seeming reluctance was actually just her getting distracted by a book.

"So, just to be clear," says Lizzie, "You've been dating this girl officially for less than two weeks, and already you've planned dates involving running, yoga, and basketball. Who the fuck are you and what have you done with my lazyass roommate? I'm not sure I like what's happening here."

"Uh, hi, maybe you should start the harassment with your boyfriend—how are his personal training sessions with Mase going?" I shoot back.

Cait cracks up, then tries to smother it in a pretend coughing fit. Lizzie sticks out her tongue, and Cait dissolves in laughter again. "Oh, come on. It's really cute."

"The two of you are an infection," Lizzie says flatly. "Leave me and my sedentary people alone."

"Are you not pleased with the results?" Cait demands.

"I'll be more pleased when I don't have to listen to reports of how much Connor's benched every day." Lizzie sighs. "We have a perfectly good exercise regimen of our own happening, thank you very much."

"Please stop there." Cait shoves one last bite of salad into her mouth, then picks up her tray. "I have to run to a study group, but I'll see you tonight, Frank? Come over around seven and we can all walk over together."

"Sounds good. And just so I know for outfit purposes, this is the one with the hoop, right?"

Cait narrows her eyes at Lizzie. "See? This is what you encourage."

I just smile sweetly, and we both wave goodbye as Cait huffs out a sigh and walks out.

"Someday, you are going to tell roommate-in-law stories that are going to sound remarkably like mother-in-law stories to everyone else," Lizzie muses.

"I'm just gonna give Cait credit that she hasn't set fire to my bedroom for dating her roommate yet."

"It's only a matter of time, though, isn't it?"

"Oh, absofuckinglutely."

• • •

True to my word, I show up to Cait and Samara's room at seven. Well, it's closer to seven thirty, but apparently Cait had planned for exactly that. It's almost as if she knows me. "Look at you, all sporty-like!" she says cheerfully when she opens the door and takes in the sight of me in my most casual jeans, a plaid button-up, and a beanie perched on my brown waves. I didn't bother with any makeup other than eyeliner, mascara, and lip-gloss, and the chalk has pretty much entirely washed out of my hair, so I sincerely hope Sam likes the natural look. "I barely even recognized you for a second."

"Decided to try something different," I say with a smile, stepping inside. "Where's Sam?"

"Bathroom, drawing Radleigh Rs on her face, like a good fan."

"Is that a subtle hint?" Cait shrugs, and I roll my eyes. "I'll be right back." I go down the hall to their bathroom, and sure enough, there's Samara standing in front of the mirror, rubbing at a smudge on her face.

She looks hella cute in ripped jeans I've never seen before, a long, cozy-looking sweater, and a sporty, stick-straight ponytail hanging down her back like a golden ribbon, and I can't resist coming up behind her and planting a kiss on her bared neck. Unfortunately, she's so intent on drawing on her face that she completely misses me in the reflective glass, and jumps about a mile in the air when I do.

"Oh my God, Frankie." Her hand flies to her chest as she catches her breath. "You scared the hell out of me." Her eyes dart around. "What if someone else was in here?"

"*I'm* in here," I remind her. "I can see no one else is. Relax."

She doesn't respond. It's pretty clear she's still a little pissed, but Cait's waiting for us, so whatever her problem is, it's gonna have to wait. Her face is a mess now, and I reach for a paper towel, wet it, and murmur, "C'mere, lemme fix you."

I can tell she wants to resist, but she doesn't; only one of us literally has face-painting on her resume, and unless we want to be late, she's gonna have to relax and trust me. It takes a couple of minutes, but I get her cleaned up and brandished with new, perfect Rs on her cheeks and put a matching one on mine, and then we rejoin Cait and get our asses to the gym.

The walk with Cait is perfectly fine, but as soon as we get to our seats, Sam gets weird again. "Maybe Cait should sit in the middle," she suggests just loud enough for me to hear.

"Seriously? You don't even want to sit next to me now?"

Her cheeks redden. "It's not that I don't *want* to, but..." She gestures around.

Whatever it is I'm supposed to be noticing, I don't. "But...?"

Cait tears her eyes off of where Mase is standing at the Radleigh bench, talking to a bunch of players, and glances at the two of us. "Everything okay?"

"Fine," Samara says cheerfully, dropping into her seat. I do the same, and so does Cait, which puts me in the middle and keeps Sam two seats away from her apparent security blanket.

Or maybe she just really *doesn't* like the natural look.

Thankfully, Cait knows the guys sitting in front of us, and she draws us all into an easy, chatty conversation that lasts until the game starts. Well, maybe Samara isn't quite as chatty in it, but it definitely distracts from whatever's going on between us—or isn't. It's tempting to ignore it completely, to fix my eyes on the court and let myself just appreciate the plethora of cut, sweaty biceps flying in front of me, but then I remember what Sam said when she came to my apartment—about being a grownup and actually talking about shit—and I soften.

It's too noisy to whisper anything to her, but I pull out my phone and motion for her to do the same. *Are you really so upset at me for kissing you in an empty room?* I text her.

She shakes her head and starts to respond aloud, then turns back to her phone instead. *No, I'm just nervous. Again. Sorry.*

I glance over at her, and holy shit, she's not kidding; the hand holding her phone is shaking.

Did something happen? And then I realize. *Did you talk to your parents?*

Slow nod.

My heart starts a heavier pound in my chest. Thirty days. We said thirty days. What happened to thirty days?

About us?

She shakes her head, and my shoulders relax. "Just stuff," she says quietly into my ear.

I'm not sure what that's supposed to be mean, but she doesn't look like she plans to type any more, and this clearly isn't the venue for any kind of conversation. She does, however, relax in her seat and shift a little closer. It's barely an inch, but actual proximity isn't the point, and I feel the rest of the tension I'm carrying slip away as we finally sit back and enjoy the game. I don't go as far as to hold her hand, but every few minutes, I brush her fingers with mine, just to let her know I want to.

Tingles—every fucking time.

Radleigh wins, and I swear, no one in that gym is more excited than Cait. She lets out an ear-splitting whistle when the buzzer sounds at the end, then grabs me and Sam and pulls us down toward the court. Mase has one hell of a smile, and it's big enough to light up the entire room right now. Cait explained to us on the way over that the basketball team's never beaten this particular rival before, and it looks seriously excellent for Mase as their relatively new student-coach for this to have happened under his tutelage.

He's talking to the other players and accepting back pats and high-fives all over the damn place, but as soon as he spots Cait coming over, he turns away from the other guys and accepts a leaping hug from her as if she's the MVP of the night. The whole team erupts into whistles and catcalls as Cait pulls him down for a huge, proud kiss, and I can't help grinning at how atypical this is for my typically PDA-hating BFF.

I'm not gonna lie—they make love look pretty damn good.

A voice from the crowd on the court calls my name, and I swivel to find the source, only to see an ecstatic-looking Jake Moss come sweep me up in a hug.

"Glad you got to see one hell of a victory," he says, squeezing me tightly before depositing me back on the court.

"I'm glad I did too! You guys kicked ass out there!" I smack him on the butt. "That's the correct move, yes? I just wanna make sure I'm sports fan-ing right."

He laughs. "Yeah, that's it. Nice job." Then he turns to Samara. "Hey, I'm Jake. You look familiar."

"Samara." She sounds a little on edge, and I wonder if she thinks Jake and I are flirting. She recognizes him all right—as Cait's boyfriend from last semester. But she doesn't know the story behind that relationship, and unfortunately, this is neither the time nor place to tell her. "I'm Cait's roommate."

"And now you're with this one, huh?" he says with a grin, gesturing at me. "Careful—she's trouble. Though you probably already know that."

Samara freezes so fast, I swear I can actually feel the frost radiating from her skin. "I'm not—no. It's not like that."

The smile on Jake's face dims a little. "Oh, uh, okay. Sorry. I thought—uh, never mind. Anyway, I should get back to the locker room. I probably stink. Good to see you again, Frankie. You too," he adds to Samara before disappearing into the crowd.

"I should get out of here, too," she mutters, already walking. Practically running. I grab Cait's shoulder, tell her we had to go, and then chase after Samara into the street.

By the time I hit the pavement, though, she's nowhere to be found.

She *can't* have gotten far. "Samara?" I call out, but there's no response. I try again, then pull out my phone and call her.

The ring is faint but I definitely hear it. When it stops, I call again, and follow the sound around the side of the gym.

Samara's sitting behind the building, hugging her knees to her chest, breathing so deeply I think she might be hyperventilating.

I drop to my knees in front of her, dead leaves crunching under my weight. "He's gay, Sam. And not out, obviously. It was just like recognizing like, that's all. I promise, there's no neon sign hanging over our heads."

The frantic breathing stops, and confusion dawns on her face. "Jake? But he's Cait's ex. He—" She breaks off, I'm guessing because of the *get there faster* look on my face. "Oh. God. She was his beard?"

"I knew I liked you for your brains."

She smiles faintly, and I need to touch her so badly, my skin is tingling with it.

"Come over, okay?" I ask quietly. "Just us."

"I can't."

I take a deep breath and sit down next to her, the cold of the cinder block wall seeping through my flannel shirt. "What happened, Sam?"

"It wasn't anything like you're thinking," she says softly. "Not like the last big conversation with them or anything. I mean, yeah, they still want me to date that Cornell guy, but it was more just...all of it." She turns to me. "This is happening, isn't it? You and me. We're going to make it thirty days."

I nod slowly. "I think so, yeah. I mean, I want to."

"So do I. And it's not like I don't want to—I've *always* wanted to—but I guess it's just hitting me now what it'll mean when we do."

"Oh, Sam." I reach out and cup her soft cheek in my palm, a moment too late to realize I'm probably smudging my careful handiwork on her face. "We don't *have* to change anything before you're ready, okay? If you need more time..."

"I appreciate that, but something tells me our 'closeted dates' aren't quite as great for you as they are for me."

I know I should make a joke then, about how having her tongue down my throat every night this week has actually been pretty damn great, but I can't make myself. The truth is, the itch to get back to my old life is surfacing little by little, not because I don't love all the time alone with Sam, but because I'm starting to feel like I'm losing myself to it. I love dancing, and I haven't been to XO in weeks. I haven't hung out with Abe or Sid or anyone else other than Cait and Lizzie outside class. And digging out my gym clothes in order to find more subtle ways to hang out with my girlfriend? It's exhausting.

But what choice do I have?

"So now what?" I ask.

"I don't know."

I swallow around the lump in my throat. "Do you need some time apart, maybe? If this is going too fast for you..." I can't even finish the sentence. I don't know how to go any slower than this. I barely know what I'm doing as it is. But I don't want us to be done.

"Sometimes I think I do," she says, and I can hear in her voice how much that confession pains her.

"And other times?"

"Other times..." In the little bit of light afforded to the night by brightness streaming through the windows up near the top of the building, I see her chew on her lip while her gaze drops to the collar of my shirt. "Other times I swear I am addicted to you," she says in a breathless whisper that turns me to liquid. "The way I think about you is, like, depraved."

"There's nothing depraved about being sexually attracted to someone, Sam," I tell her softly. "I know you've been raised—"

"It's not that," she says quickly, her soft ponytail swishing from side to side as she shakes her head. "I don't mean it in a 'girls liking girls is sinful' kind of way."

"Okay, so then what?" She doesn't answer, so I softly add, "It's just you, me, and the sky here, Sam; everyone else is gone. Remember what I said before? If you want something, ask for—"

I don't even get to finish my sentence before her mouth lands on mine, hungry and searching. It's the first time she's ever instigated a kiss like this, and it's so hot I think my bones might actually be melting beneath my skin. I crawl into her lap to get closer, the warmth from her body more than making up for the chill of the night. Especially when her hands grip my waist and begin a slow slide upward to my breasts.

I realize immediately she's never done that before, either. Even now, her touch is hesitant, as if measuring to see if it's okay. I arch forward into her palms and roll my hips against hers to tell her it's plenty good, and she gets the message, squeezing and rubbing her thumbs over my nipples until I swear they're going to rip through the flannel. "This," she says breathlessly as our hips rock into each other on another squeeze. "I swear, I have a thirteen-year-old-boy obsession with your boobs. I can't believe you don't notice how often I stare at them."

I want to tease her but I'm just too fucking horny. "They're all yours," I tell her, letting them graze her chest as I lean in to kiss her jaw, her neck, her collarbone. "Enjoy the fuck out of them. I know I am."

She groans and her fingers move from cupping my breasts to unbuttoning my shirt. "I've wanted to tear this open since the second I saw you in it," she confesses. "Even while I was freaking out in the bathroom. That's how hot it looks on you."

"Mmm, good to know." I kiss her again, then sit up straight in her lap. "And how does it look off of me?"

"Way too good." She buries her face right between my breasts and I laugh, but it tapers off into a moan as she leaves a tongue-sweeping kiss on each one of my rose tattoos. "I'm a pretty big fan of this ink, too, in case that wasn't clear."

"I got that," I manage to breathe, just as she tips me back and sucks a nipple right through my bra.

It's so unexpected, I can't help the muttered *fuck* that flies out of my mouth, and she immediately pulls back. "Oh, hell, did I hurt you?"

"Uh uh," I assure her before taking her lower lip between my teeth. "Trust me, everything you're doing is utterly fucking perfect." A little too perfect, honestly; I'm pretty sure if we keep this up, a whole lot more clothing is gonna come off. Despite how desperately I wanna come, I know that between her panic and mine, the thirty-day rules are good ones. And while the lines of what's technically fucking may be a little blurry when you're both girls, for the first time in my life, I'm going to err on the side of caution. "We should probably stop, though, because we're about five seconds from me no longer knowing how to."

"Oh God, I'm sorry, I—"

"Shh, I'm not." I kiss her lips gently as I start rebuttoning my shirt. "This is all good, okay? All of it. *We're* good."

She nods. "Okay."

We're quiet as I finish getting redressed, and then we head back out in the night, one last squeeze of our hands behind the building before we let go for the rest of the walk back.

chapter eleven

I'm groggy as hell when I wake up in the morning, which I can only blame on the fact that last night got me ridiculously keyed up. I'm so on edge with this no-sex thing, I've killed the batteries in my vibrator. I'm resorting to nineteenth-century masturbation. Whatever Carpal Tunnel Syndrome is, I think I might actually have it.

At any rate, it takes me a moment to realize that there are signs of life in my apartment, just outside my bedroom door, and another to realize it's not Connor Lizzie's talking to; it's Cait. I step into the living room and wave with one hand while covering a huge yawn with the other.

"Francesca! We were just talking about you!" Lizzie greets me cheerfully.

I wipe my eyes, still blurry from sleep, and see them seated at our little round dining table, their egg white omelets making clear Cait's the one who made breakfast. "Well, that sounds ominous."

"Not at all," Cait assures me, tipping her plate toward me in silent offering. I shake my head and go for the coffeemaker instead. "You'll like it."

"Now she won't, just because you told her she will," Lizzie says with a grin.

Cait rolls her eyes. "She's not you."

"*She's* right here. A little info, please?"

"We're gonna have a dinner party!" Lizzie smiles brightly, like we are people who have dinner parties. "You've been having trouble coming up with dates that balance actually being date-y with the fact that you guys aren't 'out,' right? So this is perfect! Plus, it'll be a good chance for the rest of us to get to know Samara."

"You know Samara, Cait. She's your freaking roommate. You see her more than I do."

Cait snorts. "First of all, no I don't, and not just because I stay at Mase's a lot."

"Well, you're still the only one of us who's spent the night with her," I grumble into my favorite *Sailor Moon* mug.

Lizzie raises an eyebrow. "Wasn't that your idea?"

"Doesn't mean I can't be bitter about it.

"Fair."

"*Anyway,*" says Cait, "we never see the two of you together, and frankly, we're all dying to see you in girlfriend mode, so, indulge us?"

"Do I have to cook anything?"

"Nope! That's the best part," says Lizzie. "Connor and I have been taking Filipino cooking classes online so we can do it with my brothers over break. We're gonna take care of everything to practice on you guys."

"Okay, *that* sounds ominous," says Cait. "*But*, there'll be copious amounts of alcohol."

"Provided by…?"

"Mase. He said you deserve it if we're subjecting you to this," she admits.

A little smile plays at my lips despite myself. If my friends had to practically get married to their boyfriends, at least they chose quality guys.

Wait, if they're practically married, and Sam and I do this triple date thing…what does that make us?

This is the point, Frankie, I remind myself, hiding my rising panic behind my mug and taking a long sip of lukewarm coffee. *This is exactly who you're proving you can be.*

Still, the thought makes my heart race, and apparently I'm not hiding it very well, because suddenly I feel Cait's calloused hand on my arm. "It's just an idea, Frank. We don't have to if you're not into it."

I force myself to relax, though it's made much easier by Cait's touch and Lizzie's suddenly serious nod. This is why these girls are my best friends—even practically married, even as awkward as it would be for

Cait, they would never give me shit for fucking this up. "No, I want to," I say, mostly meaning it. "It sounds like fun. I mean, not the part about eating Lizzie's cooking, but the rest."

"Oh, fuck you."

I blow Lizzie a kiss, which she catches in the air and then smacks against her ass.

"So, we're really doing this," says Cait. "We're having a triple date. We are all coupled. That is madness."

"I feel so adult," says Lizzie, sitting up straight in her chair. "First a super healthy breakfast with no fat or flavor, and now this."

"Hey!"

I roll my eyes. "It's an egg white, Cait. It barely even counts as food."

Cait sniffs. "Well then, if you feel that way, it's a good thing Lizzie's doing all the cooking."

"Aw, Caity J, don't worry—you can totally pick out the vodka." I pause. "Wait. Maybe lemonade. Or iced tea. I keep forgetting Sam doesn't drink."

Lizzie's eyebrows shoot up. "You're with someone who doesn't drink?"

I raise one right back. "Have you seen her legs?"

"Aaaaand that's about all the objectifying of my roommate I can handle for one morning," says Cait, but she's smiling. "I'll let Mase know it's on. Friday night at eight?"

"I'll make sure Sam's in," I say, feeling the start of butterfly wings fluttering in my stomach again. *And I'll make sure I am too.*

• • •

It takes me until later that night, when Samara and I are sitting at opposite ends of the couch, our legs intertwined over the middle and our hands occupied by chopsticks and pad Thai, to bring it up. And when I do, she laughs.

"I don't know what I'm more surprised by—that Lizzie cooks or that Cait is this okay with us dating."

"Let no one say my friends aren't full of surprises." I pluck a bit of chicken from the nest of noodles and pass the takeout carton to Samara. "But they seem pretty into it."

She smiles. "They're cute."

"So are you."

Her smile widens, and she blushes and looks down into the carton, and I want to draw her so badly right now I can feel the ache in my fingers.

"Does that mean you're in?" I ask, rubbing a thumb over the velvet bone of her ankle.

"Of course I'm in. I want to get to know your friends."

There's a quiet moment then where the natural thing to say would be "and I want to meet yours," but other than the couple of friends at home I know she's in touch with, Sam's just as lone a wolf as Lizzie.

As if someone's been watching us, Sam's phone suddenly pings with a text, and we both instinctively glance at it on the coffee table and see a message from "Jenny" light up the screen. I expect her to take it, but she just turns back to the pad Thai and feeds herself another bite. "This is so much better than the one place in Meridian," she says once she swallows. "I am definitely in favor of making this a regular thing."

"Sounds good," I say, but I can't stop looking at her phone, wondering why she doesn't want to answer the text with me here. It's not that I'm jealous—I know Jenny's just a friend—and maybe she's just being polite, not answering texts when she's with me. If anything, I should appreciate it. But for some reason, it's making me feel weird. Like maybe she so badly doesn't want our worlds merging that she can't even acknowledge a text from someone in her straight outside world when she's lying here with her long, gorgeous legs all tangled up in my super queer ones.

This was your idea, my stupid brain reminds me in a voice that's way too similar to Lizzie's. *You have no one to blame but yourself.* Out loud, I say, "You can answer that, you know, if you weren't because of me."

She shrugs. "It's just Jenny."

"Isn't Jenny one of your best friends?"

"Exactly why she won't care if I don't answer her for a couple of hours." Sam takes another bite, then hands the carton back, but I shake my head and she puts it down on the coffee table instead. "She's probably just bored on her date." Her short pink fingernails trace the chain tattoo on my ankle, making me shiver. "I, however, am not."

This is where I should sit up and meet her in the middle and lick the last traces of pad Thai from her tongue, but I can't. Even as the question forms on my lips, I hate myself for asking it, but I can't help it. "Does she know about me?"

Samara sits up, and I miss her gentle touch immediately. "That's what this is? You think I broke your rules?"

"No! No," I repeat more calmly. "It's just...if you wanted to..."

"If I wanted to what, Frankie? You asked me not to tell my friends and family about you and I didn't. Do you think I'm lying?"

"I think I hate that my friends are getting to know you and I can't do the same with yours. I know that's my fault. I'm sorry." I sit up too and take one of her hands, and I'm admittedly a little surprised she even lets me. "I'm being a total hypocrite right now."

She smiles softly, and for the trillionth time since we met, I'm struck by how utterly beautiful she is. "You are, yeah, but I like that you care. But you know I can't do the secrecy thing like that, right? It's one thing for Cait and Lizzie to know, but to put my friends in that position when they see my parents decently often, or for *me* to worry about one of them slipping…and that's not even taking into account that I can't be sure how they'll react personally, but I suspect not well."

"I know, I know. I'm sorry. I really am. I hate this for you."

"I know." She squeezes my hand and uses it to lift herself over me until she's seated in my lap, straddling my hips, her face hovering just inches over mine. "But it has its good moments too."

The only response I can manage is an unintelligible utterance in my throat as her lips brush mine and her palm cups my cheek so gently I have to cradle into her hand to make sure she's really here with me.

It's been two weeks since I begged for thirty days and already I hate everything about it. Most of all, I hate that I still need it, that I am sitting here holding this most perfect girl, and as soon as she goes back home for the night, I'll go right back into dinner party panic. Not because of her or because I don't want this—God, how I want this—but because I am clearly just fucked up.

"Do you lose yourself this deeply in thought when you're making out with everyone, or am I just especially boring?" she teases, though I'm not really sure she's teasing at all.

I reach up to tuck a loose strand of blond hair behind her ear. "You're the only person I think about too much to lose myself in."

She pauses, tips her head to the side. "Okay, that was pretty smooth."

"Enough to earn me another kiss?"

"Maybe just one." She wraps her arms loosely around my neck and brings her mouth down to mine. Beneath her, I am melting, and I wonder if I'm wrong, if tonight will be the night my brain finally settles into smooth sailing—and kissing—for the next two weeks, two months, two years. Kissing her now, it seems impossible to ever give this up.

It isn't just the way she feels, or smells, or tastes; it's the way she sighs into my mouth, like: finally. Like: you found me. Like: this is everything I dreamed it would be.

How do you ever stop kissing a girl like that?

Maybe it's just that simple, you idiot, I think as our tongues sweep over each other in lazy, relaxing rhythm, low tide on a calm day. *You don't.*

chapter twelve

I'm not sure who's more nervous for this dinner, me or Lizzie. I've been ordered to stay out of the apartment while she gets everything ready, so after work, I have lunch with Samara before logging some time in the studio. But now I'm smeared in paint and pretty desperately need a shower, so Lizzie's just gonna have to deal.

"You're not supposed to be here!" she yelps as soon as I close the door behind me. I see immediately why she's panicking—the apartment is an unholy mess.

"Just need a quick shower and a change into dinner-appropriate attire," I say, holding up my hands. "But..." I sniff. "What burned?"

"Ah, that would be the toasted coconut, I think," says Connor, "but it might be salvageable. Just a little crispy."

"Is 'crispy' another word for charred?"

Before Lizzie can respond, a beeping noise sounds from the oven, and she races toward it, flecks of batter flying off her tank top. Connor doesn't look much better, dusted with flour and elbow deep in vegetable peels. I take that as my cue to get out of the way, and in no more than twenty minutes, I'm clean, dressed, and getting shoved back out the door with soaking wet hair and a makeup-free face.

I grumble all the way back to Cait and Sam's room, but the last vestiges of my annoyance melt away when Sam pulls out a hairdryer, sits me down in her desk chair, and proceeds to work through my damp tangles with a gentleness that makes me purr.

Which is probably what makes Cait declare that she's gonna go to Mase's and meet us at the apartment.

To Lizzie's credit, when we arrive at the door to the apartment an hour later, it smells like heaven. The butterflies in my stomach momentarily get distracted by the scent of spicy fried food, but I'm brought back to reality by a gentle squeeze of my fingers.

I don't have to ask Sam if she's nervous; she's radiating it. I turn and take her other hand, a weird, indefinable ache cresting in my chest as I look at her. "Hey," I say softly.

She smiles. "Hey."

I'm wearing wedges and she's wearing ballet flats, which means I'm the perfect height to kiss her, and I do. "This is gonna be fun. Probably."

"You are not the greatest at inspiring confidence," she says, but she's still squeezing my hands, so I'm thinking I don't actually suck at it. I don't get to respond, though, because the door flies open and all five feet eleven inches of Cait Johannssen fill the frame.

"I told you guys I heard people making out!" she calls over her shoulder.

Samara turns bright red. "We weren't—"

I shove Cait's shoulder and she laughs and steps aside to let us in. The air is heavy with the delicious smells of spice and fried dough, and my stomach immediately rumbles in response. Connor and Lizzie are in the little kitchen, and they wave hello before quickly turning back to whatever's sizzling on the stove. Mase greets us from the dining table, which has the little bistro table from the patio shoved up next to it. He's pouring wine into glasses, and without missing a beat, he switches to a bottle of cider for the last glass. Next to me, I feel Sam relax a little more.

Yes, our friends are nice, I say with a squeeze of my hand.

They really are, she says with a squeeze of hers.

"Fuck!" Lizzie yelps, making both of us jump, and I look at her just in time to see something go flying from a pan. I open my mouth to ask if she's okay, but before I can, she looks over at us and her eyes widen.

"Are you guys holding hands?" Lizzie squeals. "Oh my God that is afuckingdorable."

"Lizzie," Cait warns sharply.

"What? They're cute!" She bends to check something in the oven, then curses and changes the dial. "I'm allowed to say when they're being cute."

Connor shakes his head wearily and flashes us an apologetic look. "You know, Frankie, I'm still thinking about your art show. That was really impressive."

Much as I appreciate his effort to change the subject from spotlighting me and Samara and our now awkwardly clasped hands, this one isn't much better for me. "It was no big deal."

"Oh my God, are you kidding?" Samara turns to me, fixing me with an intense gaze. "Frankie, it was brilliant. How can you say that was no big deal?"

"She always does," Cait says dryly. "You'll get used to it."

"Someday they'll ask Frankie to paint over the ceiling of the Sistine Chapel and all she'll say about it is, 'Whatever, Michelangelo's dead so they clearly just picked some rando'," Lizzie adds.

I can't help laughing, even through my blush, but Sam's still looking at me with a mixture of sadness and horror. "Do you really not get how talented you are?" she asks in a soft voice that stirs up an ache somewhere I didn't even know I had feeling. Suddenly, this is too much and I need to breathe.

160

"I save my cockiness for other skills," I say, planting a loud kiss on her cheek. Thankfully, she flushes with a shy smile, breaking the little bit of tension. Which is of course when Lizzie says, "Aw, you guys are, like, puke levels of cute."

"Dinner had better be really good if we're going to endure this much harassment," I warn Lizzie with narrowed eyes.

"Some of it definitely is," she says confidently.

"I assume we're just not supposed to ask about the rest?" Mase frowns down at the wine glasses. "Maybe we should start here."

"Solid plan," says Cait, coming up behind him and snaking an arm around his waist to get a glass. They hand them out to the rest of us. "Should we toast to something?"

"To Lizzie's cooking skills," I say quickly before any of them can try to center me and Samara again.

"Hey, just Lizzie's?" Connor protests.

"Sorry, sorry—to Lizcon," I amend.

"Lizcon?" Connor wrinkles his nose. "That sounds like a gathering of people who dress up like reptiles."

"Agreed," says Lizzie. "Cozzie is a way better portmanteau."

"Cozzie is a pretty great ship name," Samara agrees with a nod.

"Ship name?" Mase looks at the rest of us like we're speaking in tongues.

"You know, like couple names," says Sam. "Like, y'all are obviously Case." She gestures between him and Cait with her cider glass. "Or Mait. I guess both work."

"Ooh, or Claw!" Cait wraps an arm around Mase's biceps and looks up at him adoringly. "I know I said I'd never get used to people calling you 'Law,' but this actually makes it seem worth it."

"I'm suddenly vastly aware of how much estrogen is in this room," says Connor.

Lizzie raises her glass. "To my occasionally sexist boyfriend! Who, to his credit, totally cooked and cleaned today."

"To occasionally sexist Connor," the rest of us declare over his protests, then drink. I let my gaze stray to Samara's throat as she swallows her cider, then up to her mouth pursed on the cup. She catches me watching her and bites one of those pink-glossed lips.

Yeah, okay, I can make it through this dinner.

"Okay, sit! Sit! Max designed us place cards," Lizzie says proudly.

"Max is her youngest brother," I explain to Samara as we take our seats at the little bistro table, leaving the normal-size seats to Lizzie and the above-five-ten crowd.

Her lips twitch. "Cute."

"So tell us about what we're eating," says Cait as she refills her wineglass. "It smells awesome.

Decidedly *not* like it follows my diet plan, but awesome."

"Yeah, you're welcome for not feeding you steamed green beans and a chicken breast exactly the size of a deck of playing cards, or whatever," says Lizzie as she walks out of the kitchen holding a platter of what look like fried dumplings. "Trust me, pinsec frito are better than whatever kale smoothie you were planning on having for dinner."

"I believe it," I murmur. "They smell amazing."

"They better, seeing as they took forfuckingever." She puts them down in the middle of the larger table, and Connor places a bowl of dipping sauce next to them. "I was not blessed with dainty chopping hands."

"Good thing they have other uses," I say with an obnoxious wink at Connor as the rest of them help themselves. Mase passes me the platter and I hold it out for Sam before helping myself to one of my own, followed by a dollop of the sweet and sour sauce.

"Damn, these are really good," says Mase. "I gotta admit, I did not know you could cook."

"She seduced me with bacon mac 'n cheese, in fact," Connor says warmly.

"Is this crab *and* pork?" Cait asks. "God, you're trying to kill me." Not that it stops her from taking another one.

As everyone gushes over the food—with good reason; it is *damn* good—I watch Sam take her careful little bites, daintily cut by knife and fork. It honestly didn't even occur to me to use flatware, but everything she does is controlled, pristine, polite.

What if she's like that in bed, too?

Fuck.

What if we're not sexually compatible? What if she insists on eye contact at all times and calling it "making love"? She's an amazing kisser, and she didn't exactly seem restrained that night behind the gym, but making out is making out—what if sex is a whole different ball game?

"You okay?" she murmurs in my ear, breaking the anxiety spell. I blink and realize her plate is empty, and everyone else is taking seconds or thirds and listening to Lizzie and Connor talk about their Filipino restaurant tour of the city this past summer. Which gives me a brief flash into my own upcoming NYC trip, with my art history class. I hadn't thought of bringing Sam with me; hell, I hadn't thought of being tied down for that trip at all…

I realize she's still waiting for a response, and I say, "Yeah, fine," while squeezing her knee, though I'm not sure if it's to reassure her or myself. Then I join in the conversation like an actual human, and when the pinsec frito platter dwindles to nothing but flakes of gold, I jump up to help Lizzie serve the next course.

At least she doesn't notice I'm being a total space case; she's too distracted by her own cooking. "Fuck, I think I burned the garlic in the chicken and pork adobo," she mutters as she pushes a dish around in a pan. "Does this smell burnt to you?"

It kinda does, but it also looks delicious and I have no doubt she worked her ass off on it, so I just say, "Nah, it smells great."

She perks up and hands me a huge bowl to put it in, then reaches down into the oven to pull out a platter of what I know from her mother visiting freshman year are lumpia. My mouth waters in Pavlovian response to the sight of them—the ones her mother brought that first Parents Weekend were afuckingmazing—and it makes my heart ache to think about how hard this must be for Lizzie, what kinds of memories this must be bringing back. I put down the bowl of slightly burnt-smelling meat and give Lizzie a quick one-armed squeeze around her shoulders. She responds with a kiss to my forearm, and then she gets back to work, so I do too.

Connor comes in then to spoon steamed rice into bowls, and while the two of them flirt, I let my gaze travel back to the table as I finish filling the bowl.

Sam looks happy. Comfortable. I mean, she should be—she's just talking to her roommate and said roommate's boyfriend—but...it's nice to see her looking so settled with my friends, in my apartment.

Nice and scary.

Cait was clearly born for monogamy. She and Mase had barely been back together two minutes when they decided to spend a month of the summer together at their old camp. And Lizzie just cares that she's getting laid regularly; that it's constantly with the same person doesn't seem to faze her at all.

Could we actually be that, me and Sam?

Do I wanna be?

The thought clings to me as we bring out the rest of the food—the chicken and pork adobo, the platter piled high with lumpia, bowls of steamed rice, and an amazing-smelling vegetable stew Lizzie explains is pinakbet, made with about a hundred substitutions because the produce selection around Radleigh is seriously lacking. I take my seat next to Sam and kiss her smooth cheek, hating myself for having so many conflicting thoughts when she's being a perfect date at this perfect meal.

"What was that for?"

I shrug. "I like you." That, at least, I know without a doubt.

That shy smile I know so well spreads across her face, but any response she might have is cut off by the bowl of pinakbet being passed to her. Everyone takes food while Lizzie answers questions about it and accepts compliments, and I take a ton of everything, possibly burnt garlic and all. I'm just lifting a forkful of pork belly to my lips when I notice Cait and Mase out of the corner of my eye—she's daintily putting okra from her pinakbet on Mase's plate, while he puts his tomatoes on hers.

Clearly I'm not as subtle as I think, because she catches me watching and laughs. "When you spend a month living out of a camp cafeteria together, you pick up a whole lot about each other's food habits."

"I think that's an automatic thing you pick up when you've been dating a while no matter what," says Connor, then pauses. "Or maybe Lizzie's just really, really clear on what she doesn't like."

"Green pepper, red onion, black olives, cottage cheese, and cilantro," Cait and I chorus, and everyone else cracks up. "Maybe it's not just a dating thing," I concede with a grin.

"I can't think of any foods I know you don't like," says Sam, cutting a piece of chicken into even smaller bits.

"That's because there aren't any," Lizzie assures her before I can say a word, and it's true; I'm not exactly a picky eater. "Unless you count Cait's healthy shit."

"Oh my God, must I always be a target?"

"Yes." Now it's me and Lizzie who are a chorus. Cait sighs.

"Food tastes is definitely one measure of coupledom," says Connor, "but I've always thought there was something so official about knowing each other's middle names for some reason."

"I love how confounding that made it for you that I don't have one." Lizzie's smirk is the dictionary definition of smug.

"Of course you do."

"Hey, I learned how you take your coffee. That's a pretty big relationship step," she counters.

"Yes!" Cait squeezes Mase's arm. "The first time Mase brought me my exact regular smoothie order in camp, that was totally my 'oh my God, he is really my boyfriend' moment."

Mase laughs and shakes his head. "Man, I wish I could stop ruining these memories for you, but it was that kid who made the smoothies who knew your regular order, not me. You know he had a huge crush on you, right?"

Her affectionate squeeze turns into a whack on his biceps. "Seriously? First the stars and now this? I swear, our whole relationship is a lie."

"Oh, come on. Isn't it the thought that counts?"

"It totally is, man," Connor agrees.

"Thank you." Mase fist-bumps him across the table, and Lizzie and Cait both roll their eyes.

"Thank *you*, Frankie," Lizzie says, looking from me to Samara, "for not adding any more testosterone to this group."

"I'm guessing the training sessions aren't helping with that particular problem?"

She snorts, and Connor pouts, earning him a kiss on the cheek.

"Feeling a little left out here," Samara declares. "There are training sessions available for significant others of the three musketeers? I want in."

"Oh, it's just weightlifting," says Connor. "Nothing remotely as strenuous as dealing with these three all together."

"Lord, if only there were such a class," Mase adds, then ducks as I pretend to throw my lumpia at his skull. As if I would waste it. I take a huge bite instead.

So good.

Conversation turns to Mase and the basketball team, and since I know less than nothing about sports, my brain tunes out again. As I stuff my face with chicken, pork, vegetables, and rice, the earlier conversation drifts back to me.

Samara doesn't like: coffee (too bitter), black licorice (same), Jell-O (the consistency weirds her out), bananas (literally anything about them), or alcohol (doesn't like feeling fuzzy-brained).

Her middle name is Jane. She doesn't take coffee at all (see above); green tea is her caffeinated beverage of choice. Tea, period, is probably her favorite thing on earth, and lately she's taken to drinking it with one orange teabag and one vanilla teabag, because she read it in a book she loved and thought it sounded delicious.

I love that I know all this.

I hate that I know all this.

I hate most that I'm still having these arguments with myself in my head.

Fuck this. I can worry about the future later. I'm here with Samara now, and my friends—our friends—now, and I'm being a selfish asshole, all because… what? Because an incredibly sweet, smart, gorgeous girl and I might like each other too much? Yeah, my life is really terrible.

I turn back to my plate, and realize it's empty. I'm not usually a stress eater, but it helps that the food was seriously kickass. "Hot damn, Lizzie B. That was *good.* I really wish I'd known to wear sweatpants to this dinner."

"Oh, you better not be done, Missy. Any of you." She glares around the table at everyone's empty plates. "I busted my ass on dessert."

"There's dessert?" Cait groans. "Do you not even care about lacrosse season?" She pauses for a beat. "Wait, don't answer that."

"I can't imagine eating any more this week," says Mase, which earns him a withering glare from Lizzie. "But, uh, obviously I'm gonna."

"She's going to kill me if I don't, right?" Sam whispers in my ear.

"Oh, yes. Surrender is not an option."

"I might need to borrow a pair of those sweatpants."

Fucking A, the image of her swimming in my sweats is so cute. She may be a little taller, but I'm considerably curvier from top to bottom. Much as I love her form-fitting yoga wear, there's something way too irresistible about the thought of her in my clothes. "You are more than welcome to my pants anytime," I tell her, my lips close enough to graze her earlobe.

Her responsive flush turns me to liquid. Everywhere.

I need to get up from this table before I say and do things to her Lizzie and Cait have told me repeatedly should not be done in front of others.

Presumably, Samara has the same idea, because we both get up at that moment to clear the table. Everyone pitches in, and in minutes, the sink is full of dishes, and the table's covered in paper plates and plasticware (we only have so much of the real stuff), awaiting the final course.

Dessert, it turns out, is basically an entire other meal in itself. There are more lumpia—sweet ones this time, filled with banana and dusted with sugar, and apparently called turon—and a pudding of sorts she calls maja blanca, which looks to be coconut and corn, among other things. "There's also ice cream to go with the turon," she adds, reaching into the freezer, "but I wasn't feeling that ambitious, so, you guys better like Ben & Jerry's."

"Who doesn't?" asks Sam, and I know she'll happily eat scoops of it plain, since there's no way she's touching banana. (No pun intended.)

"Will you still kiss me after I eat this?" I ask once we're all seated with dessert on our plates, tapping the crispy wrapper.

She pretends to think about it while she digs a spoon into the maja blanca. "That might depend on whether I'm even able to move after I finish."

"Fair point." Like everything else, dessert is delicious, although Connor was right earlier that it was the toasted coconut that got a little charred. By the time we're all done, everyone is groaning out their compliments to the chefs, and I'm feeling endlessly grateful that I'm already home and don't have to roll my ass outside right now.

It's on the tip of my tongue to offer Samara the same fate, and then I remember: be good. I may think I'm too full to fool around right now but I suspect that can be far too easily fixed by a single flick of her tongue over my bellybutton ring—something I learned the hard way the other night.

Luckily, Mase saves the day. After everyone's lingered for a while, polishing off the wine and cider and cleaning as much as can possibly be done without actually doing our dishes, he offers to walk Cait and

Sam home. I'm surprised when Lizzie sends Connor with them, but then I see her make a subtle head tilt in my direction, and I realize she wants to talk. I cheek-kiss everyone goodbye except Sam, who gets full-on mouth-to-mouth once everyone else is out the door, and head back to the kitchen.

"So?" Lizzie asks.

"So, that was truly excellent. You guys seriously outdid yourselves."

"Not the food, you dork." She tosses me a dish towel, then runs the sink and grabs the first plate. "Look, I know you think I'm totally chill about my relationship and everything, but I have moments of terror too."

That genuinely *does* surprise me. "Really?"

"Yeah, really." She scrubs at the first plate hard enough to take off the glaze. "I think...I think Connor's it for me. Like, I actually think this might be forever. And that scares the shit out of me."

I exhale deeply. "Oh, thank God. I mean, not about the forever part—I'm just gonna pretend you didn't say that—but the scared part."

"You know me, Frank. You really think I planned to find my life partner at nineteen? You don't think I expected to be sowing my wild oats alongside you until my tits lost their perkiness?" She hands me the dish she just cleaned.

"You do have great tits."

"Why thank you." She takes another towel and snaps it at my ass, then picks up another dish to wash. "It's normal to be nervous. But you seem to really like her. And more importantly, *I* like her."

I know she's joking, but the truth is, it does make me fizzy with happiness to hear that. I know how much it means to me to like Connor and Mase, not just for my best friends but on their own. The fact that Lizzie and Cait like Samara *is* a pretty big deal.

"I *do* really like her," I admit, and it feels good to say it aloud. "I'm pretty fucking crazy about her, in fact. I don't know why that doesn't make me feel more settled."

"You'll get there," she says, giving my shoulder a squeeze with a soapy hand, then handing me another plate. "You guys are really good together. The more time you spend with her, the more you'll realize there isn't an alternative to being with her that's better than the reality you have." The corners of her lips twitch. "Unless the sex sucks."

My heart thuds. "Do you think it will?"

"Jesus, Frankie, I was kidding." She pauses. "Wait, do *you* think it will? Is that why you're so freaked out?"

"Maybe? I don't know." I put the dry dish on the counter and take the next one she hands me. "Judging by the stuff we've done so far, hell no; I have zero complaints. But sex changes things. Sex with a virgin *definitely* changes things. It's been a long time since I was someone's first."

"Well, then, don't hang too much on the first time. You've got as long as you need to get it right. Who has a great first time, anyway?"

"Uh, you said your first time with Connor was the best sex you'd ever had."

"Hello, I'm trying to be sympathetic here?" But a goofy smile steals over her entire face, and she washes the next plate with a little swing to her hips.

I throw my dishtowel at her face.

chapter thirteen

There's a week and a half left until the thirty days are up, but that's not the countdown my art history class is interested in. With midterms behind us, the trip to the Met in three weeks is pretty much all anyone can talk about. Including Abe.

"We're rooming together, yes?" he whispers to me as Professor Richter switches on the projector to show us a series of slides featuring the work of female manuscript illuminators from the 11th and 12th centuries. Excited as I am for the trip, I also actually want to pay attention to this lecture, because this work is cool as hell, especially for the time.

"Yeah, of course. We'll talk about it later." I nibble on my pen cap as I wait for the first slide to show up, wondering if I should've brought my laptop in for this instead. I generally keep it old school so I have the freedom to doodle in my margins or whatever, but unfortunately, I don't write nearly as fast as I draw.

"I think we need two more people if we want one of the cheapest rooms, right?" he continues as if I haven't said a word about tabling this. "Who else do you wanna add?"

"Not sure," I mutter, scribbling down whatever I can about Ende and the Gerona Beatus; Professor Richter will make the presentation available after class, but she always says far more in class than she ever puts on the slides. I learned quickly that her forgiving my lateness that first day was a minor miracle; the woman takes attendance—and punctuality—seriously.

"What about—"

"Abe, seriously, not now, okay? We can get coffee after class and talk about it then." Shit, I missed whatever Richter just said and now she's moved on to Diemud.

He groans, and I honestly can't believe Richter doesn't hear it, because he sounds like a fucking earthquake to me. "Tell me this isn't because you're bringing your *girlfriend* along."

He says "girlfriend" how I imagine a normal person might say "syphilis," but even more appalling is that fact that I definitely did not tell him about Samara; as per our rules, I haven't told anyone at all, other than the obvious. "What are you talking about?" I mutter, keeping an eye on the slides.

"Oh, please—you haven't been showing up to XO or any parties in weeks. I got curious. So sue me."

"You got curious so you *what*, Abe?"

Whoops—*that* might've been a little loud. Richter stops talking and her gaze flickers up in our direction. She doesn't need to say a word; her glare speaks a thousand. Thankfully, Abe finally learns to shut up and opens up a new document on his laptop instead. *God, nothing as creepy as you're making it sound. I saw your roommate and pretended I knew something was going on between you and someone, and she assumed you'd told me. JUST LIKE I WOULD HAVE.*

The all-caps are a nice touch.

FYI, that's still creepy, I scrawl in my notebook, pissed now, *and if there was something to tell you, I would have.*

So the girl's not coming? he types, completely ignoring everything else.

Of fucking course not.

I don't even hesitate before writing the response, but it does make my stomach churn a little. It's been a couple of days since the dinner party, and between how well it went (minus my own freakish panic) and my conversation with Lizzie afterward, I've been feeling surprisingly calm about my relationship—or almost-relationship, I guess—with Samara. So much so that I actually have imagined inviting her along once or twice. She mentioned having been to New York City once in high school and having loved it, but not having had a chance to go to any museums. I have no doubt she'd love the Met, and maybe the Frick even more so. It's shockingly easy to imagine walking through the galleries with her, hand in hand, talking about the different paintings and sculptures, seeing her face light up the same way it did at my art show.

But with all the other upheaval, the last thing I need is some shitshow with Abe. Sam and I still have another week and a half to get through, anyway, and who knows where we'll be by the time the trip hits. Inviting her is dumb; if things go south between now and then, this will just make it a million times worse.

At any rate, Abe seems mollified, which means he's finally quiet and listening to Richter. I turn back to the presentation, only to see that a slide about Herrad of Landsberg is now up on the screen. Fuck. What happened to Diemud? And did I miss anyone in between?

All I can say is we better find more people to room with for the trip, because at this point, leaving me alone with Abe might be a recipe for murder.

• • •

For all that I'm kind of a mess about the Samara stuff, I've also learned nothing soothes me faster than curling up with her and watching something mindless on TV. I hadn't planned to see her that night, but with the stress of my argument with Abe weighing on my shoulders, I knew she'd be exactly the fix I need. Month-ago Me is laughing her ass off at how content I am right now in another girl's bed, all our clothes on and a movie we're actually (mostly) watching on the screen. But I feel good. Happy.

Which makes it a good time to finally take a little baby step forward.

"So, thirty days is coming up," I say, toying with her fingers as I try to ignore the familiar pressure in my chest. "What should we do to mark it?"

The slightest smile plays at her lips, and she bites one to stifle it. Winged creatures that could devour butterflies whole take flight in my insides. What I wouldn't do to take the hand currently in mine and put it where I could get a little relief from what that smile does to me. "Besides that," I say, knowing it'll make her blush. It does.

"I was thinking dinner, maybe," she says, her eyes fixed on our hands in my lap. "Kind of a redo of our first date. There's a Middle Eastern restaurant in Meadowbrook that I've been wanting to try—it looks like the closest to Armenian food I'm gonna get around here, and Lizzie inspired me to want to show you my food. I'm pretty hopeless at cooking without my grandmother, though, so this is the best I can do. And I know you have to work the next morning, so maybe we wait one more day and do Friday night instead?" Her face takes on that pretty pink flush I love so much. "For, um, sleeping-in purposes."

"I love that idea," I tell her, leaning over to kiss her on the nose. "It's a date. I'll ask Lizzie for her car."

She snuggles in even closer, and I kiss her again, this time just behind her ear. Then at the curve of her jaw. I love the way her inhalations go shallow as I suckle gently down her throat, nibbling and tasting her smooth skin until I reach the neckline of her tank top, and then I kiss along that, too.

"You are really good at that," she breathes, her nails digging into my back.

I tug down one of her tank top's straps with my teeth. "Just you wait."

"What if I don't want to?"

I freeze, my lips still pressed to the fine bone of shoulder. It's an easy question, despite the slow and steady throb between my thighs. I slide up on the bed so I can look her in the eye while I cup her cheek. "Then we won't. Not until you're ready, Sam, okay? However long that takes. You are so worth waiting for."

"I appreciate that," she says, grazing her thumb over my bottom lip before leaning over and nipping it between her teeth, "but I meant what if I don't want to wait anymore?"

She closes the distance between us before I can manage a response, her warm mouth sealing over mine while her cool hand slides up my T-shirt. I instinctively wrap a leg around hers to pull her close and slip my hand beneath the waistband of her yoga pants to cup her ass. I'm surprised when my fingers encounter nothing but skin, meaning she's wearing either a thong or nothing at all. Both possibilities are hot as fuck.

She moves to lift my shirt over my head and I let her, then do the same with her tank. The little green lace bralette she's wearing underneath doesn't leave much to the imagination, but it *does* bare a whole lot of smooth golden skin. I retrace my path down her jawline, her throat, her collarbone, but this time, I don't stop. Her breath hitches as my mouth grazes a nipple through the lace, and I linger there while my fingers go back to teasing at her waistband.

Thong.

Desperation to see her in nothing but these little scraps of fabric washes over me, and I kiss my way down to my fingers and sit back on my heels to tug her pants down.

And then the sound of banging at the door startles me off balance, and I topple off the bed just as Sam's RA's nasal voice calls, "Hall meeting in five minutes!" through the door.

"Frankie!" Sam gasps, and I mutter out a curse and rub my bruised butt. When I look up at her, she's trying not to laugh. She fails, but so do I. "I'm so sorry," she says, offering me a hand. "I completely forgot that was tonight."

She pulls me back onto the bed, and we're both still laughing as we find our shirts in the tangled sheets. "It's probably for the best," I say as I pull mine over my head. "We're still not at thirty days."

"This is true."

I brush my lips over her forehead. "But good to know you're ready."

She smiles sheepishly. "You too, I guess."

As I watch her fix her hair into its default smooth ponytail, I can't help feeling grateful for the interruption. Yes, physically I am so, so ready to have sex with Samara, my clothing is about to spontaneously combust. Any concerns I might've had over whether it'll be good seem like the worries of a very, very silly girl.

Emotionally, though…I still wanna wait. I know it's just a week, but it's the principle of the thing. I want to know I can do this; no, I want to *have done it*. For maybe the first time since we got together, my hesitation isn't because I'm afraid I can't commit.

It's because I finally believe I can.

"I'm gonna see if Sid and Lili wanna have dinner, but I'll text you later." I kiss her again, full on the mouth this time. "And I'll see you bright and early in the Psych building."

"The last time there I won't be able to kiss you hello," she muses as she slides her feet into flip-flops.

I imagine it—a good-morning kiss to start my day twice a week—and I really, really like the way it looks in my head. "The very last," I say as I give her one final kiss goodbye and slip out the door.

• • •

As day thirty nears, then passes, my confidence remains blissfully intact. Admittedly, I owe that in part to none other than romance guru Elizabeth Brandt, who's been giving me pep talks on demand. For the big night, she goes a step further and gives me a Xanax, just in case there's any lurking creature of panic somewhere in my brain.

With an hour left to dinner and the pill working its magic, I'm pretty calm...but I'm also dressed with nowhere to go just yet. Sam's study group went late, and she asked if we could meet here to drive over at eight, instead of seven as we'd originally planned. But in the interest of keeping my shit together, I'd already mentally arranged my whole day for being ready now, and an added hour alone with my thoughts is *not* what I need.

A walk, I think in a flash. Perfect way to clear my head, take in the changing leaves and whatever instead of the fact that I'm turning in my bachelorette card. I know the fresh air and some time alone will help, so I double-check my makeup, throw on a coat, and head outside.

There's no particular destination in my mind, but out of habit, I find myself wandering toward Greek Row. Given how many times I've forgotten my troubles in one of the fraternity or sorority houses, it's only natural that's my compass's True North. But it's confirmed that I made the right decision when I get to the actual street and sniff.

Barbecue.

I fucking love barbecue.

Best part? It's clearly coming from the Sig Psi house, where I happen to have an in.

"Frankie! Long time no see." Doug Leach's smile when he sees me picking my way up to the front porch in my boots is big and genuine and at the sight of it, I'm reminded of all the fun, casual, no-strings-attached times we've had in this house. How weird to see him and have him be off limits. And how do I tell him that *I* am? Especially after over a year of telling him I'm not interested in relationships or anything more than a good time?

"Hey, Doug." I accept a kiss on the cheek hello. "I was passing by on my way to dinner and saw the house was hopping. Figured I'd come say hi and see if I could mooch a bite of your hot dog. And no, that's not a euphemism."

He grins. "For you? Always. You can have a whole one, if you'd like."

I should definitely say no—I'm going out to dinner—but they smell so damn good. "Just one," I say, but then I quickly amend it to half; I know it's important to Sam that I eat at the restaurant tonight, and I need to make sure I have room.

"Tell you what—I'll split a hot dog with you if you buddy up with me for flip cup. I need your magic hands."

I know he's flirting, but flip cup sounds like the perfect thing to soothe my addled nerves. Plus, Doug is an actual good guy, not the type who thinks he's automatically entitled to my body because he's been granted entrance before. "Deal, but I have to be in Meadowbrook by eight. Do *not* let me lose track of time."

"Scout's honor."

"There is no way you were a scout," I say, even though he is absolutely the type.

"You win us flip cup, I'll tell you whether I was or not." He waggles his eyebrows and I laugh, and we head inside.

For all that I'm not terribly athletic—my sporting experience starts and ends with joining the neighborhood softball team for two years to meet girls—I am damn good at this game. I pound my beer and flip my cup in one perfect shot while their first guy is still chugging. "Damn, you are impressive," Doug says affectionately as I down the celebratory Jell-O shot he brings me when we win. "Do you want another hot dog? You've earned it."

"I can't," I say apologetically. I've heard enough about Sam's love of dolma and nazook to know I should be saving belly room. "I really do have to run."

"Oh, come on," Charlie, one of the guys we just trounced, says, wiping a dollop of ketchup from his burger off his face. "You have to give us a shot at a rematch."

"Can't just embarrass dudes on their home turf like that," another guy, Marcus, adds.

I glance at Doug, who's already setting up eight new cups, and sigh. I know I should go, but after tonight, when I'm officially done with Doug, these guys are gonna like me a whole lot less. Sam wouldn't begrudge me having fun with them one last time, right?

I'm back at the table before I can even contemplate the answer to that question.

This time, I'm a little less impressive. The guys put me third for strategic reasons, and by the time I lift the cup of lukewarm beer to my lips, I'm feeling a little out of it. I don't chug it nearly as fast, and as my team chants their encouragement, it echoes in my head with a pounding pulse. I finish anyway, and it takes me seven or eight tries to flip my cup. When I finally do it, I nearly keel over.

"Hey, you okay?" Doug asks from his starting spot.

"I'm fine." I wave my hand to let him know not to worry, but I nearly smack myself in the face. "On second thought, maybe I need to sit down."

He guides me to the couch, and I feel myself getting sleepier with every step. "Dude," I say quietly, and am I slurring? "What the fuck is in that beer?"

"It's just beer," he assures me. "We all drank the same stuff."

"The Jell-O?"

"Just vodka. Nothing weird."

I nod, feeling like a puppet. I trust Doug, but more importantly, I can't think anymore. I just need to close my eyes for a minute, and I'll be fine.

Just a minute.

chapter fourteen

I wake up feeling like death, and my mouth tastes like I've been making out with a raccoon. Blinking down at my body, I see I've definitely fallen asleep in my clothes. And not just any clothes, but actual nice ones—my best jeans and a wrap top I usually reserve for holidays at church, though I wear it with a tank top underneath for that and right now I am definitely not. In fact, my boobs are pretty nicely displayed right now— or will be, once I retie it properly—which is exactly why I picked this top for my date with—

No.

No no no no no.

My head whips around to take in my surroundings, and I get so instantly dizzy that it takes me a full minute to realize where I am.

In Doug's room at the Sig Psi house.

With sunlight streaming through the window.

Which makes this...the morning *after* my big date with Samara.

The date I never showed up to.

Holy shit. I am a monster.

I rub my eyes until I can actually see clearly, and that's when I realize I'm alone in the bed. I look down at the floor, and there's Doug, curled up with his head on a pillow, sleeping like a baby. The bed belonging to his roommate, Jorge, is mercifully empty, though the clock on the nightstand says 10:42 a.m., so for all I know, he slept here last night with us. It's not like I remember coming up here, and I certainly don't remember crawling into these sheets.

What the fuck happened last night?

I slip out of bed and look at myself in Doug's grubby mirror. My shirt may be askew, but it's still tied, the edges of my black lace bra peeking out from underneath. My jeans are still on, zipped and buttoned. Whatever went down last night...well, it doesn't seem like anything did, literally or figuratively. I don't even have any beard burn on my face, and considering Doug only shaves like once a week, that's pretty telling. The only clothing I'm missing are my boots, and those are easy enough to find on the floor.

So again, I have to wonder...what the hell?

Unfortunately, my pounding headache makes it hard to think, but a quick search of Doug's toiletry bag yields a bottle of Advil. It's only as I'm pouring three into my hand that I finally figure out what happened to make me lose my entire night.

That fucking Xanax.

How could I have forgotten I'd popped one of Lizzie's pills to keep myself calm for my date? And *how* could I have forgotten that Xanax—especially in the dosage she's got—and alcohol do not fucking mix? So now, basically, I've combined chemical coping mechanisms only to screw myself into the worst, most stressful situation of all, because I am an asshole and how the hell am I supposed to explain to my girlfriend—if I even still have one—that I was *so* nervous about a date I should've been excitedly counting down the minutes to that I stupidly knocked myself into a coma?

I grab my phone from my butt pocket and light it up.

Shit. Three missed calls. I check my texts, and sure enough those are full too.

Hey, are you in there? I've been knocking for a few minutes already. Time: five minutes after eight.

Ten minutes later: *I'm guessing you're not in there, and my feet are starting to hurt from standing in your hallway. I'm gonna head back to my room and wait for you there, OK?*

Ten minutes later: *I called the restaurant and moved our reservation half an hour, but that's the latest they'll seat.*

And finally, when there's been no response from me for an entire hour: *Guess you're not coming. Hope everything's okay.*

That's it. And it only takes a minute of scrolling through the texts to figure out what's bugging me about them. There's nothing from Lizzie, nothing from Cait. If Samara were really worried that something had happened to me, she would've contacted them. Or maybe she did, but *they* weren't worried. Either way, however well I've been thinking I've been concealing my anxiety…clearly, I haven't been fooling anyone. And that knowledge just makes everything worse.

How did I ever think I deserved her?

No, fuck that. I'm not giving up that easily. I fix my shirt in the mirror, use Doug's toothpaste and deodorant to make myself a little more human, pull on my boots, and do the best I can to clean up my hair and makeup. Even if I've burned any chance I had with Sam, she deserves better than to think I don't give a shit, that I just didn't show up because I don't care. She doesn't have to forgive me, but she does have to know how sorry I am, and, yeah, maybe how crazy I am about her too.

Because I am. Because I *wanted* to be there with her last night. Because I want to be with her now.

I slip out of Doug's room and out the door of the Sig Psi house, ignoring all the whistling trailing after me. I'm still feeling a little dizzy, and it takes me a minute to orient myself, but finally, I manage to pick my way over to Wilson Hall.

Where no one answers when I ring up.

I step away from the security desk and dial Samara, but it rings three times and goes to voicemail. Not that I'm surprised she's screening my calls. I don't bother trying again, and instead call up Cait. That one doesn't even ring, which means she's probably in the gym. I could go there and drag her back here to bring me up, but before I do, I try Sam again. And again. And again.

No luck.

The gym it is.

• • •

By the time I let myself into my apartment, I'm physically and emotionally exhausted from searching for Samara on every square inch of the Radleigh campus. I can't blame her for not picking up her phone any of the billion times I tried her, but even Cait has no idea where she is. I am completely at a loss.

For now, I just need to be patient, recharge, shower the smell of the Sig Psi house off my skin, and then figure out how to make the world's most epic apology.

No problem.

The place is quiet when I close the door behind me. "Lizzie B.?" I call out as I hang up my leather jacket on the hook by the door. "You here?"

Silence.

I walk further into the apartment and spot a note on our little round dining table. *Have fun,* it says in her scrawl. *I'll see you tomorrow.*

Clearly Lizzie's in her own universe; "fun" is the last word I'd use for what lies ahead. I drop her note back on the table and continue on to my room, grumpily throwing open the door.

And there, lying on my bed, hair fanned out around her, fingertips dangling over a book she must've dropped to the carpet in her slumber, is Samara.

I'm tempted to pinch myself to make sure she's real. How long has she been here? And what—

Wait.

I blink, and blink again. I was so startled and relieved to see her when I first walked in that I didn't even notice what she's wearing. Or isn't wearing. One of those long, golden legs is adorned with an honest-to-goodness lacy garter. A garter that matches the lacy frills emerging from a skintight pink satin corset rising and falling with every one of Samara's delicate breaths.

She is fully decked out in the most fuckhot lingerie I have ever seen.

I want to wrap her in my arms, bury my nose in her hair, and kiss her senseless so badly it aches. I want to stare at her in that outfit for days, want to peel it off in seconds, want want want.

But I haven't earned it, haven't earned her. She deserved so much better from me, and I don't know why she's here now, but I know I need to make her stay.

I glance at the book on the floor—is that flower on the cover supposed to look so vaginal?—and then back at Sam. She hasn't so much as stirred since I walked in. Kissing her awake seems too presumptuous, so I kneel by the bed and lift her fingers to my lips instead. Her eyelids flutter open, revealing those gorgeous tiger eyes that melt me every time, and I say, "Hey."

She blinks and I wonder if I should take back my hand. I don't know if she's here to read me the riot act; I don't know how to reconcile her being here with what happened last night at all. But then her lips curve into a slow smile and she says, "Hey," and I leave my hand wrapped around hers.

"I've been trying to call you."

"I've been asleep, apparently."

"How long have you been here?"

"Since...ten, maybe? Eleven? Lizzie let me in, then said she was going over to Connor's."

Samara's been here for *hours*. I've been chasing her all over campus and she's been *here*, waiting. For me. For this. For whatever's coming next. "Sam, I am so, so sorry about last night, and this morning, and...everything." I squeeze her hand and use it to pull myself up so I'm sitting on the bed at her knees. "I hate

195

myself for not showing up, especially because I *wanted* to show up, but I was so nervous that I took one of Lizzie's mega-Xanaxes, and then suddenly I was waking up in—"

I cut myself off, but she doesn't miss it. "Where?" she asks quietly, and I know she's been wondering this since long before I opened my mouth, since long before I even returned to my room. "Where did you wake up this morning, Frankie?"

There's no way to make this sound good; all I can go with is the truth. "With Doug, at the Sig Psi house."

She sucks in a sharp breath, but doesn't say a word.

"Nothing happened with him, Sam. I promise you. And you don't even have to take my word for it." I reach into the back pocket of my jeans for my phone, hit Play on the voicemail Doug left me at some point during my rabid campus search, and then hit the speakerphone.

"Frankie? Hey, where'd you go? I woke up and you were gone before we could even talk. And listen, I just want to make sure you know nothing happened last night. I don't know why you were so out of it after a couple of beers, but I put you to bed as soon as you passed out. Can you just, like, let me know that you're okay? Okay. Thanks." There's a long pause and then a breath that suggests he's gonna speak again, but instead, he hangs up.

Samara presses her lips together. "He sounds like a good guy."

"He is."

"But nothing happened."

"Nothing but a text back to tell him I'm okay."

"And are you?"

It's a loaded question, but an easy answer. "I am now."

That finally gets a smile out of her. It's small, but it's there, and I'll take it.

"So...this outfit," I say, my voice turning raspy as my gaze flickers over her body, lingering on the small, perfect breasts pushed up by the boning of the corset, the curve of her hips underneath the second-skin satin. "Did you wear it here to seduce me or destroy me?"

That tiny smile turns sly as fuck. "Can't it be both?"

"I think it must be. You look like an angel sent from hell." I glance down at the scrap of lace encircling her thigh. "I have to admit, if you left me alone here right now, it would be some well-deserved revenge." I dart out my tongue to wet my lips; my mouth is desert dry. "Cruel and horrible, but deserved."

"Do you *want* me to go?"

My eyebrow shoots skyward. "You're kidding me, right? I've been looking for you for hours. All I've wanted to do since the minute I woke up this morning—since the minute I saw you for the first time, really—is be with you, preferably in this bed. I don't want to do anything *but* this, like, ever again. I just feel shitty about it happening after last night."

She curves her palm around my jaw and leans in, but she doesn't brush her mouth against mine. Instead, she takes my lower lip between her teeth and bites down, tugging until I groan with the pleasure and pain of it. "Here's the deal, Francesca," she says, her voice so low I have to strain to hear it. "I made a decision this morning that I would hear whatever you wanted to say. And now, it's my turn to get what I want."

"Anything," I say, and I mean it with every fiber in my being. "What do you want, Sam?"

A lone fingertip grazes my forearm, tracing the ink there, the lines from a classmate's poem I had tattooed there last semester. *This is the story of a woman who had done it all wrong.* "I want what I came dressed for. So, is that still on the table?"

A rush of warmth floods my body, every nerve cell pinging. "If you still want me then *yes*. Hell yes. Yes, yes, yes."

The last yes isn't even fully out of my mouth before she swallows it in hers, burying her hands in my hair and pulling me back to the bed with her. I surrender completely, letting her take control of this kiss, of anything she damn well pleases, knowing it's only a matter of time before the roles are reversed and she's melting under me instead.

But she isn't giving up control just yet. Her hands yank open my shirt and push it from my shoulders, her nails raking my back on the way down. We're only half on the mattress, kissing too hungrily, too desperately to care. I hate that we could've been doing this all last night, that we *should've* been, but I'm here now, and so's she, and all of it feels like such a miracle I could kick myself for ever doubting this.

"You're thinking too much," she murmurs, shifting back on the bed, then tilting her face up for another kiss, which I gladly relinquish. "We don't have to do this if you don't want to."

"I want to," I tell her. "So fucking much."

"Well, it's mutual." She rises to her knees and puts her delicate hands on my shoulders. "So why are we still talking?"

I want to speak, but I can't. It's as if she reached into my chest cavity and squeezed my heart in her little hands. But she's right.

We don't need to talk anymore.

I bury my hands in her hair and close the distance between us, the distance I never want there to be again. She walks back on her knees without moving her mouth from mine, and I follow until she's lying back against my pillows and I'm above her, tasting, touching, inhaling her honey-citrus scent until it's imprinted on my brain.

She's so soft—her lips, her skin, that fucking lingerie. I kiss my way to her jaw and suckle down her throat, every one of her breathy sighs and moans hitting me where it hurts. My jeans are the denim prison of romance novels, but I can't make myself stop touching her long enough to take them off. I slide my hands down her fine-boned shoulders to the perfect handfuls of her breasts, and she arches into my palms with a gasp.

The sounds she makes are the sexiest part, a constant reminder of how new this is to her, confirmation I can make her feel damn good. I hear it in her whimpers when I drag my tongue along the edge of the cups of her corset, her groans when my thumbs seek out her nipples through the satin and she unconsciously rocks her hips against mine. But I want more, always more. She is so beautiful and lying right here for me and I don't want her covered by my hands, by my body. What a waste.

Suddenly, I'm struck with inspiration. I pull back reluctantly and give her lower lip a little love bite before sitting up and climbing off the bed. "Come here."

She blinks up at me dizzily. "You want to go somewhere now?"

"Just trust me."

She takes the hand I hold out to her and stands, letting me drag her over to the full-length mirror in the corner of my room. I wrap my arms around her from behind and press my lips to the back of her shoulder, our eyes meeting in the reflecting glass. "Look at you," I rasp, taking her in from her beautiful blond head to the pink nail polish on her perfect little toes, and every satin-and-lace-wrapped curve in between. "Look how fucking stunning you are. I didn't want to miss it."

She doesn't say anything, though she flushes in some choice places, and I smile against the back of her neck before covering it with gentle kisses. My arms are still around her, one hand over her heart, feeling her pulse race beneath lazily trailing fingers.

And then I slowly trace my tongue down her spine.

"Oh, God," she breathes, her eyelids fluttering shut.

"Keep them open. Watch me."

She does. She opens her eyes and fixes them on the reflective glass as I suck her neck while I palm her breasts, squeezing gently, then not so gently. Every now and again, she sways on her feet with a moan, but I keep her steady and watch her watching me.

Then I slide a hand down down down the smooth satin. Her breath hitches as I trace a finger along the smooth strip of skin between her corset and matching panties, and I force myself to be patient, even though every ounce of my being is dying to know if she's as wet as I think she is. "Sam?" I whisper, still kissing whatever skin I can reach—shoulders, arms, that long, slender neck.

"Touch me," she whispers back without hesitation. "Please, please touch me."

Jesus fucking Christ. My hand obeys as if of its own volition, sliding beneath the waistband, and oh my fuck she is soaked. My fingers glide right over her clit, and she trembles under the touch.

I maneuver her forward until we're so close to the mirror her breath is fogging the glass, and she puts her hands up on the walls on either side of it to brace herself. A little of the tension drains from her body, but only for a moment before I slide my hand back through her wetness, grazing her clit in light circles.

"What are you doing to me, Francesca?" she utters desperately as I stroke harder, faster. "How can anything feel this good?"

"Oh, sweetheart, you have no idea." I slip into the cup of her corset, gliding over the softest bare skin, and squeeze, aching to feel her nipples hard and tight against my palm. She doesn't disappoint, arching with a whimper while my other hand speeds up over her clit. I want to be inside her, want to devour her, but I wouldn't change what we're doing right now for anything. Not with the way her eyes have gone wild, or the way her moving with my hand has her ass grinding against me. Not when her golden skin is growing flushed and damp, her hair mussed just enough to suggest she's been gently fucked. "This is only the beginning."

As I say the words, though, I realize they're not true. This isn't the beginning. I've been crazy about this girl for months. I've been dreaming of touching her like this since the moment I saw her a year earlier. This started so long before now, and there is a lifetime left to go.

But right now? I want to see her finish.

I slip down further, sliding a finger inside her easily, though she's so tight a second would probably be a stretch. She sucks in a sharp breath, and I grind my palm against her clit until she gasps out a moan that turns me to liquid. I keep my eyes on the mirror, progressively gentling the hand fucking her until her cries and shuddering taper off into a whimper. Then I ease out, missing her soft, wet warmth the instant I've lost it.

"Oh my God," she whispers. Her knees are buckling, and I squeeze her tight to hold her steady. Once she's focused again, I wait until her eyes are watching me, then suck my finger down to the last knuckle.

"Francesca."

I keep her staring at me until I've licked off the very last trace of her. "Yes?"

"I am going to pass out."

I smile and draw her back to the bed, aglow in the presence of her complete and total contentment and the knowledge I'm the one who put her in that state.

I'm also horny as fuck.

She looks like she wants to sleep for a year, so I debate leaving her for a few minutes to take care of myself, but before I can even open my mouth to suggest it, I feel a light touch grazing my belly, then a gentle tug at the button of my jeans. "May I?"

Two softly spoken words and I am on fire, arching off the bed into those delicate hands. I watch her slender fingers work the button, then the zipper, and then she's between my legs, tugging the jeans down and off.

On her knees, her blond hair streaming over her shoulders, she makes a gorgeous picture I'll recall on many future lonely nights. Only one thing could make her more perfect right now. I sit up, brushing my lips over hers while my hands snake around her back to the tips of the ribbon keeping her corset in place. "May *I*?"

"Uh huh."

I do, and the garment falls away, leaving smooth golden skin and small, beautiful tits in its wake. I press a kiss to each while my fingers dance up her spine, and her body shuddering under mine is exquisite.

I could keep going like this for hours—touching, kissing, tasting, sucking—but Samara clearly has other plans. She pushes me back to the pillows and follows me down, her tongue sweeping over my lips. I reach up to cup her head so I can kiss her more deeply, but she slips out of my grasp before I can, kissing my neck, down my throat, along my collarbone.

I let my eyelids flutter closed as her lips continue downward, over my breasts and down my torso in slow, luxurious kisses that spare no tongue. She may never have done this before but her every move exudes a confidence and certainty that reminds me with every touch why I am utterly crazy about her.

There isn't even a moment's hesitation when she reaches my thong and keeps on kissing the damp lace. When there's nowhere left to go, she picks her head up just enough that her breath kisses my clit through the fabric. I inhale deeply to try to stay in control, but the scent of sex is so heavy in the air I can taste it.

She hooks her fingers into the waistband and slides the thong down my legs, unconsciously biting her lip as she does. It's so fucking sexy it hurts to look at her, and I brace myself for her touch, expecting gentle, experimental.

I *don't* expect her to put her mouth right back where it was, that gentle touch courtesy of her catlike tongue instead. "*Fuck.* Sam." I grip the sheets like a lifeline, panting, my grasp on the fabric the only thing keeping me from thrusting a hand in the gorgeous hair swirling over my thighs so I can keep her there forever. "You don't have to do that."

She picks her head up, the distress on her beautiful face pinging my heart. "Am I doing something wrong?"

"Fuuuuck no," I assure her, my laugh turning breathless as she slides her hands up my thighs, her thumbs parting me, stroking with a painful slowness. "I just…if you want to go slower…"

"You really don't get it, do you?" Her eyes meet mine, and where they're usually tiger-like in color only, now they're fierce and feral. "How long I've been fantasizing about this?"

"Going down on a girl?"

"Going down on *you*." She slides a finger inside me, and my eyelids flutter closed. "Your thirty days may have been the right idea, but I've been wondering what you taste like ever since." She slides a second finger in easily, and I writhe greedily against her hand, so, so close. "So, if you want me to stop, I will, but—"

"I'm gonna come the second your tongue touches me," I warn her.

"No, you won't." She kisses the inside of one thigh, then the other, going higher and higher until she reaches damp skin. Then she touches just the tip of her tongue to my clit, and smiles. "Never has Frankie ever."

I'm so lost in my lust haze, I have no idea what she's talking about. I make some unintelligible noise.

"That first game of 'Never Has Frankie Ever.' I finally found out whether you were kidding about getting that piercing."

"Disappointed?"

"Nah." She strokes me delicately with a fingertip, her other hand moving in and out in relaxed rhythm. "I don't like the taste of metal much. The taste of *you*, on the other hand…"

There's nothing I can do but groan as she dips her head back down to circle my clit with her tongue and proceeds to show me just how much she means it. She's slow and delicate, as if she's still getting comfortable, and the feathery touches are short-circuiting my brain. I want her to go at her own pace, but the superhuman effort of not writhing against her tongue is making me break into a sweat.

Faster, my brain is screaming. *Harder. Fuck me fuck me fuck me.* I bite my lip so I don't scream it, claw the sheets so I don't bury my hands in her hair. This is heaven and hell all rolled into one, and if she were anyone else I would reach down and take matters into my own hands. But I don't want to scare her off, or make her think this isn't—

Oh, fuck, I think she figured it out all on her own.

When she picks up both the speed and pressure of her fingers and tongue, it takes less than a minute before I succumb to the mind-blowing white light of an orgasm that rocks me to my bones. When I finally sigh into nothing but a gelatinous mass, I pull her up on the bed with me and kiss her until there's nothing left of me on her tongue.

"Wow," she says sleepily as she curls in at my side. "So that's what all the fuss is about."

"Mmhmm." I can barely keep my eyes open, but the image behind my lids is pretty great.

"I think I'm a fan."

Welcome to the club, I try to say, but it comes out as a murmur as I drift off to sleep on the scent of sex and orange blossoms.

chapter fifteen

I awaken to an empty bed.

I usually do, so the realization that this time it feels wrong slams into me like a lightning bolt. The absence of soft skin pressed into my side chills me with goose bumps, and I slip out of bed and pull on a pair of boxers and a hoodie before stepping out into the living room.

It's a relief to spot Samara immediately, sitting on the sofa wrapped in a blanket and cupping a mug of what I assume is tea, staring out the sliding patio doors at the pouring rain pelting the glass. I climb up behind her and wrap an arm around her waist while kissing the side of her neck. "Hey."

"Hey. Hope it's okay I made myself some tea."

"Of course. Sorry I don't have vanilla. It's harder to find than you'd think."

She doesn't respond, and it strikes me then that she hasn't turned to look at me, let alone kiss me. She hasn't leaned into my one-armed hug, or even touched the skin wrapped around her.

New as I am to relationships, I know something's going on that is not good. "Everything okay?" I ask, even though I'm not sure I want the answer.

"Yeah. Just thinking." She takes a sip from her mug, and I wonder if it's still hot. I have no idea what time it is, no idea how long I slept, no idea how long she did. Finally, she turns around, moving out of my grip. "We should talk."

Suddenly, I envy her blanket and tea, because I am growing very, very cold. "Okay."

"I just want to say that…I'm sorry," she says, those beautiful eyes meeting mine with an unblinking gaze.

She's sorry? After I accidentally coma'd myself out of our date? "Sam—"

"No, please, let me finish." She puts her mug down on the coffee table and I think maybe now she'll take my hands, but she doesn't; instead she starts picking at a thread on Lizzie's chenille blanket draped across her lap. "I'm sorry I put so much pressure on us being a capital-T Thing. On sex. On everything. I didn't get it. Now I finally feel like I do, and I realize I've been such an idiot."

"What are you talking about?" I ask slowly. "Get what?"

"That sex is *fun*," she says with a faint smile. "That being with someone doesn't have to be this dramatic, all-serious, epic…whatever. I get why you didn't want to limit yourself to one person. And I've been putting all this pressure on *myself* to do that, too, but you never have and you…" She laughs, but there doesn't seem to be any joy in it. "Well, you've always seemed way happier than I ever have, so clearly you've had the right idea."

She couldn't have stunned me more if she'd slapped me across the face. This is everything I wanted her to feel that first night we kissed, but now? Now that I've spent the past month pushing myself toward the conclusion that she's the only one I want, *now* she wants to see other people? To *sleep with* other people?

If there's one thing I came away with after having sex with Samara, it's that I'd be plenty happy with her being the only person in my bed for the foreseeable future.

What went wrong that she came away from it with the exact opposite feeling?

"Was…was it bad for you?" I splutter, because it's all I can think, even though the words don't feel right at all. I *know* she enjoyed it, in more ways than one. What the fuck did I do wrong?

"No! God, no. Frankie. Come on. You were there, right? You can't possibly think that." She frowns. "Unless you—"

"Nope," I say firmly. "I guarantee you there are no complaints on my end."

I cannot even believe I am having this conversation. What the fuck *is* this conversation? Why are we affirming to each other that what was obviously mind-blowingly incredible sex was mind-blowingly incredible sex? Is this yet another relationship thing I was unaware of?

God, no wonder I've been so damn averse to these things.

"Okay." She picks up her mug again. I guess she needs something new to do with her hands. Funny—I thought we had some nice options covered. "It's the opposite of that, really. It's like…it opened me up." She smiles wryly. "No pun intended."

I force a laugh that would be real under any other circumstances, but this doesn't feel funny at all. This feels a whole lot like getting dumped. "So, you want to fuck other people."

Her cheeks flush, but it doesn't melt me the way it usually does; instead, it just makes me angrier. Or sadder. I'm not really sure which one I'm feeling. "I'm just saying, we don't have to do the whole 'exclusive couple' thing. I thought…I don't know what I thought, really. I guess I thought that when I had sex, that would make it official. That it would be the turning point where I couldn't hide being gay from my family and friends anymore, or something. But…I had sex. And the only person who knows that besides me is the person I had it with."

"Did you think there was some magical sex fairy who sprinkled dust on you afterward so everyone would be able to tell?"

She huffs out a laugh. "I don't know what I thought. Down in Meridian, I'm under such a microscope—everything I do is about how it reflects on my parents, my grandparents, my town. Thinking about what I want is always so tangled up in what everyone around me wants *for* me. I guess this just made me realize that this is about me, not anyone else."

"And what you want is to date around?" I clarify, trying to keep my voice light despite the stinging feeling in my chest. Because she's right—this *is* about her. She's the one dealing with coming out. As much as I hate the idea of her being with anyone else, I also don't want to hold her back because of what *I* want any more than I want her parents to.

"It's what you wanted from the beginning, right? And now you'll be free for your trip to the city."

Her voice is a little shaky as she asks, and I don't know if she's afraid I'll argue with her or what. I know that coming here against her parents' wishes was the biggest fight of her life, and she's had to do nothing but defend her choices since. I won't make myself a fight too. "Right," I say, wondering if it sounds as hollow to her as it does to me.

Judging by the way she nods, it doesn't. "Okay then." She leans over and pecks me on the mouth, then gets up with mug in hand and pads over to the kitchen to rinse it. The blanket falls back on the couch as she rises, and I see that underneath, she was wearing a T-shirt and boxers.

My T-shirt and boxers.

I'd thought the lingerie she wore last night was the sexiest thing I'd ever seen, but I can't imagine anything better—or worse—than the sight of her right now. I gaze shamelessly at her mile-long legs as she stands over the sink, and all I can think as I mentally lick them from ankle right up to the cotton hem is *mine*.

Only she isn't.

She shuts off the sink and turns to put the cup in the drying rack, catching me staring. I think she must be able to tell that I'm eye-fucking the hell out of her, but all she says is, "Oh, right. I borrowed your clothes, too. Hope that's okay."

I want to rip them off you, I think.

I want to fuck you out of them, I think.

"It's fine," I say.

"I should probably change back now anyway and head home," she says. "As long as I'm borrowing stuff, do you have an extra umbrella or baseball cap or something?"

I glance back at the patio doors. The rain has lightened up a little, I guess, but I still wouldn't want to walk outside in it. I open my mouth to tell Sam she's welcome to stay the night, but then I realize she knows that; she *wants* to leave. And I have to let her. "Sure, take whatever you need."

She disappears into my bedroom to change back into her clothes, and I busy myself with digging through the coat closet to find my umbrella. It's my only one, but I'm sure as hell not going anywhere tonight, so. I also grab her jacket, and I'm waiting with both like a human coat rack when she emerges a couple of minutes later, wearing a cute dress I realize must be concealing the fuckhot lingerie underneath. "Thanks," she says when I hand her the jacket and umbrella. "I'll return it ASAP."

"It's fine," I say, because I guess they're the only words in my vocabulary right now. "You can give it back on Monday morning."

I wait for her to say something about how it's only Saturday, how there's so much of the weekend in between now and then and she hopes she'll see me sooner, but it never comes. "Perfect."

Perfect. I think we must have very different definitions of that word.

I walk her to the door, unable to believe she's really about to leave. To go out into the rain rather than cuddling with me on the couch, watching a movie or one of her favorite cooking shows. To spend the night in her room alone instead of with me, on me, under me.

But she does. And there's nothing I can do but watch her walk out.

• • •

God bless Studio Art. I love painting here on any normal day, a bastion of peace broken only by the sounds of brush strokes and whatever music Suzanne plays at a low volume, surrounded by some combination of Sid, Abe, and Lili. But on a day like today when I truly need to feel alone but not lonely? It's exceptionally perfect.

Or at least it would be if my friends weren't so observant.

"Are you sure you're okay?" Sid asks me for the second time

I *could* say, "I'm fine," like I've been saying over and over, but apparently that doesn't help, so this time I say, "Why would I not be?"

She shrugs. "I don't know. That just seems a little…darker than your usual stuff."

I look at my work. We're supposed to be coming up with our own representations of the word "Hope." Even I can recognize that the amount of black on my canvas is a little excessive. But it's hard to feel a whole lot of hope after spending an entire weekend sitting on my ass, fielding only the super occasional text from Sam as if everything was normal and fine, then seeing her this morning just long enough for her to return my umbrella. Had I brought her tea like I'd contemplated, I probably would've ended up chugging it myself; she certainly didn't stick around by the front desk long enough to notice whether I had another cup with me or not. "Just taking a different approach."

She shrugs and turns back to her own work, which is definitely more cheerful; the swaths of saffron, emerald, and indigo are far more calming than anything I'm likely to produce today. It seems far nicer to be in Sid's brain than mine.

"Actually…" I start to speak, then hold my tongue. I haven't told Sid about Samara, and I have no idea if Abe has. Now would be a weird time to mention that by the way, I've sort of had a girlfriend for the past month, only not really, and now not at all. "Never mind."

"What is it?" she asks, turning the full focus of her gaze on me. Behind me, I hear Abe shift, and I know he's pretending not to listen even though he absolutely is.

"I was just wondering how you're doing," I say, and it's only half a lie. "We haven't talked much about the Jen breakup. You seem okay, but if you're not…you can talk about it, you know." *Please, please talk about it, because I would love to understand how you're okay.*

"Oh, you're sweet," she says with a smile that makes me feel more than a little guilty. "But yeah, it was definitely for the best. No regrets. Honestly, she and I were not a good fit. And I can't believe I'm saying this, but...I actually like Karim. Kind of a lot." She shakes her head, the sparkly clip in her hijab catching the light. "Please don't tell my parents that. Ever. The last thing they need is any sort of confirmation that they know my love life best."

"Secret's safe with me," I promise with a smile, jealousy settling deep in my gut. I'm perfectly familiar with "The best way to get over someone is to get under someone else," and I'm glad that's working for Sid— metaphorically speaking, I imagine, since I don't *think* she's knocking boots with the guy she met at the Muslim center's Parents' Weekend dinner, and to the best of my knowledge, she wasn't with Jen either—but the thought of getting with someone else now just depresses and exhausts me.

Which of course makes me wonder why it *doesn't* do that for Samara.

I feel a tap on my shoulder, and this time, it's Abe. "You still pissed at me?" he asks, keeping his voice low.

I *am* kind of annoyed at him still, but there really isn't any point; Samara coming on the trip is a non-issue at this point, and I guess I can't blame him for being a little nosy. Under normal circumstances, I'd be sharing every detail of my love life with him and Sid. "No," I grumble. "But spying on me wasn't cool."

"Agreed," he says immediately. "I really am sorry about that, and for being a dick. I just had visions of us wingmanning each other on this trip, and it never even occurred to me you didn't have the same visions. If you wanna bring the girl—"

"I don't," I bite out, realizing too late that I'm being too loud. Suzanne glances in our direction, and I mouth an apology; though she doesn't mind us talking, the volume is definitely expected to be lower. She nods and continues walking around, appraising work and answering questions. All at once, I'm reminded of that moment Samara walked into the gallery for my show, looking gorgeous enough to break every heart in the room, and Suzanne's "she looks pretty special to me."

"Wait. What girl?" Shit. Sid. I turn to face her and see she's got her free hand on her hip, a dark eyebrow arched. "Is this"—she sweeps a hand in front of my Hopeless Hope—"about a girl?"

"It's not about anything," I lie, officially over this conversation. "Bringing the girl it's *not* about on our trip was never a consideration," I say to Abe. "Wingmen forever." We fist bump into an explosion, and Sidra shakes her head.

"The two of you are gonna get into so much trouble down there, aren't you?"

"Perhaps *you* should come with us and find out," Abe suggests, waggling his eyebrows. "We *do* need more roommates."

"If you think my parents would let me share a room with a guy, you have clearly not been paying attention."

Abe grins. "Touché."

We lapse back into painting quietly, and blessedly enough, there are no more mentions of Samara for the rest of class.

Getting her out of my head, though? That's another story.

chapter sixteen

I fully expect my head to be clearer and the rest of me to be in prime wingwoman form by the time we actually board the bus to the city for the weekend, but alas, I'm every bit as single-minded as I've been since Sam basically dumped me a week and a half ago. Worse, maybe, since it's not like she's disappeared; in addition to seeing her every Monday and Wednesday morning, we've still been hanging out a little—a movie here, lunch there, and, yeah, the occasional making out, too. It feels different to me now, knowing I'm not the only one her lips are touching, wondering how many other wrist tattoos she's been tracing.

But then, I guess she's had to live with a whole lot of wondering stuff like that about me too.

The bus ride down to Port Authority is long and torturous, lightened up only by Abe's company and the occasional exchanged text with Lizzie or Cait. My fingers itch to say hi to Sam, just to check in, but I'm afraid it's too hover-y, too girlfriend-y, too all the things I'm continuously surprised to realize I want to be.

Hell, this week I actually thought about saying something, finally. I sat at the desk during her Wednesday morning class and sorted mail while I rehearsed how to say everything I was thinking in my head.

I'm actually not so into the idea of us hooking up with other people, so...can we maybe not?

I know I originally wanted us to just be casual, but it turns out my feelings for you aren't really casual at all...

I cannot fucking stop thinking about you. Are you really not thinking about me?

None of it was smooth, but none of it mattered— she walked out of class straight-up flirting with another girl, and she didn't so much as glance at me on her way out. She wasn't kidding when she said she wanted other options. And now I'm on my way to New York, a city fucking *full* of them. I need to get her out of my head.

Next to me, Abe's lying back with his eyes closed, listening to music, but I squeeze his knee until he pulls out an earbud and looks at me. "Talk to me more about what we're doing tonight," I say. "After the gallery, I mean."

He pulls the other earbud out and turns to me with his game face on. "Does this mean you're finally ready to get in wingwoman mode?"

"Damn straight."

"Fucking *finally*." He holds up his hand for me to slap, and I do, unable to stop a grin from spreading across my face. "Dude, Seth gave me a whole list of clubs to hit up while we're here. I promise, you will not leave the city in the same practically re-virginalized state you're entering it."

I'm about to inform Abe that not having had sex in a week and a half isn't exactly re-virginalization, but then I remember I haven't told him about that part of things with Samara. I certainly don't want to relive it now, so I just say "Good" and leave it at that.

Seven hours later, we're standing in the Danika Keim Gallery in SoHo with the rest of our class, our stuff stashed in the hotel room we're sharing with two classmates Professor Richter paired us with. All the sculptures on display are by female Bosnian refugees, and they're awesome—reinterpretations of famous photographs of the war—which makes it all the worse that as I walk through the solemn space, all I can think about is how much Samara would love this. Soft, phantom fingers squeeze mine, and I have to cough to relieve my throat of the scratchiness that suddenly creeps into it.

"This is so badass," Abe murmurs as we walk around, taking it all in. And it really is. I push all thoughts of Sam and everything else out of my head and focus on the art; Lord knows it deserves it. I'm focused on a particularly dark one, all sharp, jagged edges, when my phone buzzes in my back pocket. I slip it out and glance at the screen. Cait.

"I just have to grab this," I say to Abe, then motion that I'll be right outside. Once I'm on the sidewalk, I pick up. "Hey, Caity J. What's up?"

"Did you and my roommate somehow split up without telling me?"

Goose bumps prickle on my skin. "It's a little more complicated than that," I say flatly.

"Is that seriously all the information you're gonna give me?"

"Since when do you want more?" I counter. "You didn't want us to date and congratulations—now we're not. You win."

"I *want* you to be happy, Frank. So what the hell happened? Why is she going out with Nora tomorrow night?"

I freeze. That sentence hurts so much, it's like getting a full-body tattoo, minus any pleasurable undercurrent to the pain. Nora is the extremely cute goalie on Cait's lacrosse team, and I would've done unspeakable things to her in my pre-Sam days if Cait hadn't strictly forbidden it. The ugly idea that I broke

Sam in for her nauseates the shit out of me. "You'll have to ask her that."

"She didn't even tell me," says Cait. "The only reason I know is because Nora was bragging in the weight room."

"Well, she didn't tell me either," I snap. "Maybe she just prefers athletes. Or undercuts. Or girls who don't suck dick."

"Frankie!"

"What, Caitlin? What." I have *never* shed tears over a person who doesn't share my blood, but right now, they're stinging my eyes, made worse by the chilly night air. I don't want to talk about how I fucked up. I don't need Cait knowing that this is all my fault, that if I had just shown the fuck up, everything might be different right now. Because it may be true, but it hurts like fucking hell anyway.

She doesn't tell me to calm down, or ask what happened. Instead, in a quiet, measured voice, she says, "If you don't want Samara seeing anyone else, you need to tell her you don't want her seeing anyone else."

As if it's that easy. As if those are words that just roll off my tongue. Not to mention the fact that I have no right to say them. "Samara can see whoever she wants," I say as coolly as I can. "It's not like I'm sitting home alone. I'm out in the city, and trust me—my tits look excellent in this shirt. I'll be just fine."

She sighs heavily. "Frankie—"

"I gotta go. I'm with my class at a gallery. I'll talk to you later, okay?"

"Okay." I can tell she wants to say more, but thankfully, she can tell I don't want to hear it. "Have fun over there."

"Thanks, Caity J. Have fun with Mase tonight."

"How'd you know I'm seeing Mase tonight?"

I just snort. "G'night, babe." We hang up, and I go back inside, praying it's only a matter of minutes before we leave for a bar and I can get obliterated.

• • •

My hangover in the morning is brutal, and waking up to Abe drooling on me super does not help. By sheer miracle, we manage to get to the Met along with the rest of the class, but we waste far too much time in the café, reviving ourselves with black coffee while moaning about how we both feel like shit. At least Abe got some ass to show for it; I lost him for a solid hour last night while he made out with some guy at...I already forget which bar. I, on the other hand, spent my sadass night texting Lizzie and stalking Samara's Twitter feed. (No mention of a date, just some commentary on *Chopped* baskets and then a lone tweet about curling up with a book.) (God, she's so...her.) (Why do I like that so much?)

But gorgeous museums like this one are basically my mothership, so once we get enough caffeine in our systems, I manage to drag Abe around until he's finally with it too. For the first time since Samara effectively dumped me, I feel like I'm back in my element.

And then, of course, we walk out of the museum and I spot a fucking adorable middle-aged lesbian couple sitting on the steps. They're huddling together against the wind and sharing a bag of those amazing-smelling peanuts being sold from carts lining Fifth Avenue, and just like that, a wave of loss washes over me. I wrap my arms around Abe's bicep and squeeze.

"You okay?" he asks, glancing down at me.

I shrug, still clinging to him like a baby koala.

He follows my eyeline to the couple, then sighs and kisses the top of my head. "You wanted to bring the girl, didn't you?"

I shrug again, tearing my eyes away from them and letting Abe lead me down the sidewalk, past clusters of tourists, vendors selling art and food, and mustard-yellow cabs honking as they swerve around each other on their way downtown. "I'm not sure *what* I wanted." I press closer to Abe as a couple of kids pass by on scooters, whooping loudly. "First I was freaked out by the idea of a relationship, and then I kinda got into it, and then...I don't know."

"But you miss her."

"I do," I say on a sigh. No matter what else is confusing the shit out of me right now, the fact that I would kill to be hanging on her arm instead of Abe's is impossible to ignore.

"Are you gonna tell her that?"

"Nope."

He laughs. "Then let's go get food. I'm starving."

...

We eat, then go back to the museum for a few more hours, and then we go back out for dinner with a bunch of other kids from the class. Afterward, everyone discusses evening plans—bars, movies, pool hall—but while I know I *should* go with them to distract myself from the fact that Sam's on a date, I just can't. I don't have the mental energy to do anything but collapse on the bed in my hotel and sketch.

"You sure you'll be okay on your own?" Abe asks.

"No," I say honestly, "but I don't think I'll be any better surrounded by people. Go ahead. Have fun."

"Okay, but call me if you need me and I'll come running back to the hotel, all right? Oh, and don't charge porn to the room—I'm not paying for that."

I smack him on the ass and send him off to join the crowd on their way to a karaoke bar, which includes our other two roommates. As if I would ever keep Abe from karaoke.

He was obviously joking about porn, but having the room to myself for the first time all weekend does give me...thoughts. Lord knows how I'd be spending the night if I'd brought Samara, but I suspect it would involve far less clothing than I'm wearing now. I strip down to my tank top and pull on the drawstring shorts I brought for pajama bottoms, then climb into the bed I've been sharing with Abe.

(Would Samara have cared I was sharing a bed with a guy? Even though said guy only likes guys?)

(Who the fuck cares what she thinks? She's going on a date tonight. With *Nora*.)

I grab the remote from the bedside table, but I don't turn the TV on. Instead, I wonder what Samara's wearing tonight—if that pink dress is now her standard first-date dress, or if now that she's all...liberated or whatever, she's dressed like sex on a stick. Maybe they're not going out at all; maybe she's inviting Nora over to snuggle up in her bed for a movie. The thought makes me sick to my stomach.

Before I even know what I'm doing, I've pulled out my phone and I'm calling Sam.

"Hey!" She sounds surprised to hear from me, but not displeased. That's good. And I don't hear anything in the background, so I'm guessing I got her while she's still at her dorm. Cait's admonishment to be honest with her about not wanting her to go on this date is ringing in my ears, and I can't help wondering if I *could* stop her, keep her right where she is, right here with me. "Aren't you in the city?"

"I am. Just had some time to kill and thought I'd say hi." Oh, fuck it. "I saw this really cool exhibit last night and I kept thinking about how much you'd love it."

"Oh?"

I tell her about the sculptures and the stories behind them, and I'm right—she's completely enraptured. It feels oddly good to be right about that, especially when I think about how there's no way Nora would have any idea.

Take that, Undercut.

"And how was the Met today?"

"Amazing. As always. I think we were there for something like six hours."

"Oh, jeez. You must be exhausted. Or, knowing you, probably not," she says sheepishly. "What are you up to tonight?"

"Not sure yet," I admit. "But I'm feeling pretty lazy. Everyone else is out, and I'm just lying here in my hotel bed." I pause for a moment to let her consider the visual, to remember the last time she saw me lying on a bed…underneath her lovely mouth. "The rules from my roommate start and end with 'no charging porn to the room,' but, you know, we'll see."

She laughs, but it's low and sexy and I know—I *know*—her mind is exactly where I want it to be. "I'm sure you could do just fine on your own," she teases.

"You know, I bet I could," I say. "Especially with a little assistance."

She laughs again, brief and breathless. "Oh yeah? What exactly does it take to get off the girl who's done everything?"

I close my eyes and slide my hand up my thigh while I drown in her honey-whiskey voice. *So much less than you'd think.*

"I wish you were here," I surprise myself by saying, not because I haven't figured out by now that I should've invited her but because I don't need her to know that.

She could say, "I could've been." She could say, "You should've invited me, then." Instead she says, "What would you do if I were?"

Ravage the shit out of you like the wild animal you turn me into. "Pull your hair out of that ponytail."

She laughs, and I let the tip of my index finger slip inside the black lace panties I'm wearing for no one. I could paint my entire body in what her voice does to me. "You're so sure I'm wearing one."

"Yes." But I wouldn't really pull it out. I'd wrap it around my fist, yank her head back, and suck every inch of skin around the base of her throat until I left marks. "You are, aren't you?"

"Yes."

Two fingers, circling, sliding, marveling.

"Do you hate the way my hair looks up?"

"I like the way it looks swirled on my thighs better."

"Well that's a different story."

My hips jerk off the bed as I finally let my fingers graze my clit. "It's a very good story."

"You're just a sucker for happy endings."

My fingers pause in their ministrations. "That was a terribly good pun."

"Thank you. I thought so."

There's no heaviness to her breathing, nothing to suggest she's mirroring my hand on the other end of the line. She's probably sitting upright on her bed, maybe even doing her nails or something in preparation for her date. My girl is so very, very good.

And I am losing her.

The unbearably horny girl in me wants to press her to play along, ask what she's wearing, or something equally obvious. Not that the answer matters; whatever it is, I'll just picture her fingers creeping under it, stroking her golden skin. I'll wish they were my fingers, to be followed by my tongue.

But they're not, because she's there, and I'm here.

Because I'm a fucking idiot.

"Hey, you still there?" she asks.

"Always." But I slip my hand back out, wiping my fingers on my thigh. She deserves so much better than me, and now she's gonna go out and find it.

"After all this time?"

"Huh?"

She laughs. "No *Harry Potter* for you, huh?"

"Oh, no. Not yet." I have no idea why I throw on those last two words. I have no desire to read or see *Harry Potter*. But I somehow sense admitting so would be a dealbreaker.

"As long as you read it eventually. I could totally see you getting a hot 'mischief managed' tattoo."

"I have no idea what that means, but if you think it's hot, I'll certainly consider it."

"You'd do that to your body for me?"

Okay, she can't possibly expect me to keep my hands above board with that one. "Wouldn't be the first thing I've thoroughly enjoyed doing to my body for you."

"Jesus Christ, Frankie." My name ends on a soft groan.

"You brought that on yourself and you know it."

"And yet somehow, you always take it a step further than I've even imagined possible."

Before I can respond, there's a static-y noise over the phone, and then a muffled "Be right there!"

All the heat that'd been coursing through my body turns to ice. "Date's here?" I try to sound casual, but I sound like an asshole. There's no way she misses it, but she's polite enough to pretend she does. "Cait, uh, mentioned something."

"Oh, well, yeah, and somehow I got distracted

from finishing my makeup, so I'm a little bit of a mess. I should go."

There's no way she looks like a mess to any degree. I should probably say, "Have fun," but the words stick in my throat. All I want to do is ask her not to leave, to stay here with me on the phone until we fall asleep, completely spent. I want to tell her about the Met, and the adorable couple on the steps, and all the paintings I'd want her to see if she were here. I want us to watch the Food Network together and listen to her yell at the TV until we fall asleep.

I want her to be my fucking girlfriend. And I don't want to share her. Not with anyone. Not like that.

"I'm sure you look gorgeous," is what I actually say. "Bye, Sam."

A woman's voice floats back to me, obscuring Samara's, and I hang up.

chapter seventeen

The topic of The Date feels unavoidable when Samara stops by my desk to say hi on her way out of class on Monday morning, even though it's obviously the very last thing we should be talking about. I'm not proud of the fact that I'm burning with morbid curiosity about every single detail, from where they went to exactly how well the night ended. But all I ask is, "So, how was getting out there?"

Her face lights up, and immediately I am beyond sorry I asked. "It was good!" she says, and I force myself to mirror her smile. "I mean, I was still super nervous, even though I'm a woman of experience now, but she was so sweet, and it was a lot of fun!"

As I listen to her talk, new things hit me about the surrealism of this situation. Like the fact that some other girl on campus got to take Samara out on an actual *date*, not having to worry about whether anyone saw them, not having to worry if it was too obviously romantic, not having any stupid rules between them at all. It feels so fucking unfair, like I'm retroactively being judged for my painting in a contest that was actually for sculptures.

"That's great!" is what I actually say aloud, because apparently instead of her ex-girlfriend, I'm her sexual Yoda. She seems to genuinely not realize that this is all killing me, and what the hell am I supposed to do with that? "And you were okay? No parent-related panicking?"

"Some," she admits. "But it was just pizza and a movie—nothing too out there or too public. Baby steps."

She smiles sheepishly, but all I can think is, *How dare you eat pizza with someone else. That is* ours.

That's a lie. I'm also thinking, *Did she make a move on you during the movie? Did you make one on her? Did you see any of the movie at all? Or did you just have your tongues down each other's throats the whole time? Fuck, I wanna die.*

"Hey, that's a legit date. Sounds like a big step to me." *And one you should've taken with me.*

(She tried.)

(I fucked up.)

(I know this.)

She flushes with pleasure and it's all I can do not to pick up one of the files on my desk and slice into my skin with it. "Thanks, Frankie. It means a lot to me that you're so supportive about all this stuff."

"Of course."

Kill me.

"I just want you to be happy," I add.

With me. And me alone. Nora can go fuck herself. Or anyone else on campus. But you're mine.

"I know," she says softly. "And I really appreciate that." She glances around, then leans in. "Can I tell you something wild? I actually got asked on *another* date."

"By Nora?" I smile slightly despite myself. "I'm not exactly shocked, Sam."

"No, by a girl in my Political Theory seminar! I feel like I'm suddenly wearing a rainbow flag everywhere I go. How did she even know to ask me?" She frowns. "Or maybe it was just a friendly coffee offer, now that I think about it. God, this is confusing."

At that, I can't help laughing for real; she's such a fucking adorable babygay. "I'm guessing it's whatever you wanna turn it into, but yeah, unfortunately, that part stays confusing for a good, long while. Hell, I wasn't sure about you for months."

"Really?" She laughs. "God, I felt like I was so obvious around you from that very first night. I knew I was in trouble the minute we met. You make it so impossible not to flirt with you."

"Just one of my many superpowers," I reply, waggling my eyebrows.

Her cheeks turn pink as she suppresses a smile, and it feels like the sweetest little victory. "I should probably let you get back to work."

"Yes, I have very important files to...file. I'll see you around, Sam."

She flutters her fingers goodbye, and then she's gone.

On Wednesday, I call in sick.

• • •

I'm tempted to do it again on Friday, or to quit altogether, but the sad irony is that I need the money even more than I did when I first got the job, because taking a girl out on dates was definitely an unanticipated expense. Anyway, it's not like Samara's actually there on Fridays; it's just impossible to sit at that desk and not subconsciously wait to see her long legs coming around the corner. The four hours I spend there that morning feel even more interminable than usual, and everything I do to pass the time—outline my final paper for Richter, sketch, screw around on Twitter—reminds me of her.

I am so pathetic.

"You are so pathetic."

I blink up into the shadow Lizzie's casting on my face, standing over me while I lie on the couch for what could be hour two or hour seven; I have no fucking clue. She looks dressed to go out, though, so I'm guessing it's closer to the latter. "A little more sympathy and tequila, a little less stating the obvious, please."

"Is this what you pining looks like? It's gross."

"Your warmth is really appreciated at this difficult time."

She shoves me over and sits down at my shoulder. "Francesca. This is not you. Which means one of two things: either you aren't you anymore because you are actually in love with somebody, which is great, but *you need to fucking tell her*, or you're wasting the hottest years of your life wallowing over nothing when you could be getting off with some fine young gentleperson."

I know I should have some smart response to this, but Lizzie's words have struck me totally dumb. "You think I'm...no."

She snorts. "How many times do we have to do this? In the past year and a half, you have watched your two best friends in the entire world find happiness in romance. Do we make it look so fucking terrible?"

"Oh, shut up." I whack her in the face with a throw pillow. "You know that's not the issue."

"Then what is?" she asks, plucking the pillow from my fingers and tossing it on the floor.

"Well, for starters, the fact that even if I'm interested in settling down, *she* isn't. Or did you conveniently forget that part?"

"No, I didn't forget, but I also think you're giving up awfully easily. I've seen you guys together, Frank, and you are so damn happy. Both of you. I don't think you even notice how she stares at you half the time when you think she's watching TV, or hear how she talks about you like you're the most gifted artist who ever walked the earth."

"Then why—"

"Because she thinks it's what *you* want, is my guess." She sweeps a hand over my hair in one of those maternal gestures I've noticed her picking up a whole lot more in the past year. "It doesn't sound like you put up much of a fight when she suggested you see other people."

"How could I put up a fight about that at all?" I protest. "If that's what she wants, who am I to tell her she can't have it? What kind of hypocrite does that make me when it's what *I* wanted at the start?"

"Jesus, Frankie, you're allowed to change your mind. Connor did it to me about a billion times, and it was annoying as fuck, but you know what? Love is *confusing* as fuck. It's okay if you used to be scared of something you aren't anymore. You don't have to be the same person a month or even a week into a relationship; pretending other people don't change you is bullshit. When you really care about them? Of course that can change you. I know that's scary as shit, but it's not always a bad thing."

I close my eyes, letting her words wash over me. I *am* different. I can argue the hell out of that in my brain, or I can just embrace it. My father entered seminary thinking his love for God was the most supreme love of which he would ever be capable, and then he met my mother at a rest stop near Springfield and it completely flipped everything he ever trusted he knew about himself. My mother hadn't been sure she ever wanted to get married or have a kid, but being with him changed that about her too.

Let's face it—love reminding Bellisarios that we don't know ourselves as well as we thought we did is in my genes.

When I open my eyes again, I see Lizzie smirking down at me. And I reply with the first words that come into my brain: "Can I borrow that purple shirt with the non-existent neckline?"

She gets up and reaches down to help pull me off the couch. "I thought you'd never ask."

• • •

It's wrong to make Lizzie think I'm going to Samara's room, I know, but if I want to make sure Samara is really my future, I have to know that I'm ready to give up my past, first.

Inside XO, lights are flashing, Gaga is playing, and the smell of alcohol and body spray hangs heavy in the air. Familiar faces smile and say hi and give me air kisses, and glittery arms hug me, and I'm not gonna lie—it feels a little like being back home. This place has been my mothership for years in the less-than-rainbow-y rural wild of upstate New York, and I love it for the fact that it never changes.

Until I spot one very big, glaring change at the bar, in the form of the last person I ever expected to see there.

I contemplate walking over, but I can't force a single one of my limbs to move. Instead, I just watch Samara Kazarian sip from a glass while she flirts mercilessly with Lana, the pink-haired bartender who used to overdo the vodka in all my drinks. Judging by the way Sam's throwing her head back as she laughs, I'm not the only one who's been on the receiving end of this particular move. Or maybe it's the fact that I have never, ever seen her take so much as a sip of alcohol, and for all I know, this is her very first time. Which makes me wonder who she's here with—Nora or politics girl or someone else entirely—because they *better* be keeping an eye on her if that's the case.

When no one comes up to her after two minutes, bleeding into three, I start to make my way over, but she unexpectedly gets up first. And spots me. To my surprise, her eyes narrow and she abruptly turns back to the bar. She says something to Lana, and a few moments later, I watch in abject horror as another bartender—this one an unfamiliar face to me—relieves

Lana from her post so she can join Samara on the dance floor.

I realize then I've never seen Samara dance, and it's probably a good thing, because I never would've been able to go a month of abstinence if I had. Her body moves with Lana's like they've been fucking for months, and absurdly I wonder if maybe they have, if maybe everything I thought there was between us was one huge surreal joke.

She catches my eye again, and holds it as she slides her hand lower to just brush Lana's ass.

That is fucking *it*.

Before I can stop myself to think better of it, I storm over and yank Samara out of Lana's grip, into the corner of the floor where it's a fraction of a decibel quieter than where she'd just been dancing. "What the hell?"

She raises an eyebrow, which just feels like an extra layer of cruelty. I fucking love those eyebrows. "Got a problem?"

"Yeah, I do. Why the hell are you here?"

"I imagine the same reason you are," she says coolly. "This is where you come to party, right? To have fun and drink and get laid? It's obviously good enough for you to be back here, so why not me?"

"Come on, Samara. You don't want to be here. You're not this person."

"But you are, right? This is the life that's so much more compelling than one with me you can't give it up. This is who you are and need to be, right? So don't you want me to get it? Wouldn't everything be easier for both of us if we were both like this?"

Well, fuck me—Lizzie was right after all. I am so stupid. "Sam, stop. I don't want you to be anyone else."

"Oh, really? Because you seemed pretty supportive of it the morning after we slept together. You were more than ready for me to become just like you."

"*I'm* not this person anymore, Samara. *I* am fucking obsessed with a girl and haven't touched anyone else since the first time I kissed her. *I* am the fucking idiot who spent 48 hours in the city missing and getting herself off to her ex-girlfriend instead of enjoying the trip. *I* have become someone who'd rather watch the Food Network and eat pad Thai than go out and party because it means more quality time with you. I've basically given up tequila for tea because all I want is for you to be happy, so don't tell me I'm this person. I haven't been this person since I fell head-over-ass in love with you."

The entire room falls deathly silent, and my shouted proclamation rings out in the club that hasn't been my playground in a good, long while. Even the DJ's stopped spinning. Sam doesn't say a word; no one does. Not until the DJ leans forward and says into the mic, "Well, that was romantic as fuck." Then he mercifully starts the music back up.

The corner of Samara's pretty mouth curves up. "It was, wasn't it." She reaches out, taking an indigo strand of my hair in her fingers and twirling. "I haven't been trying to change you, Frankie. I never wanted to change you. Or maybe that's dishonest."

"No, I get it," I say, because I finally do. "You didn't want to change me; you wanted me to want to change." I shrug. "Well, I did change. But it seems you did too."

"I want what I've always wanted," she says, shaking her head slowly. "You. The you who is passionate, adventurous, artistic, fearless, and incredibly sexy. I don't want all that to be behind door #1 while I'm behind door #2. *You* decided I didn't mesh with your life, that I wanted you to be someone other than who you are. *You* decided you couldn't talk to me about how much you were freaking out, that you had to be finished with this place and frat parties and whatever else. But I'm not looking to cut you off from everything you love, Frankie; that's not the relationship I want to be in. I just want to be part of those things *with* you. But if I bring you down, if I change you in any way other than by keeping you monogamous, then you should break up with me."

The idea of letting her go makes my heart ache almost as much as the realization of how stupid I've been, how much I hurt the girl I love by assuming she couldn't handle or love who I am, even though she's been saying otherwise this entire time. "If I promise to stop being such a moron, can I keep you instead?" I ask, stepping closer and twining my fingers with hers. "I'm sorry. I'm still new at this. But I want you, in my life, in my world, for as long as you're willing to put up with me."

"That might be a really long time," she says like a warning.

"Good." We're standing so close right now, I breathe the word into her mouth, then wait for her to kiss me.

It's brief, just a brushing of her lips over mine, before she murmurs, "You wanna go?"

I reach out to tuck a strand of hair behind her ear, my pulse racing with want. "Uh uh."

"No?"

"How badly do you want the old me?" I whisper, my fingers grazing her jawline.

"Frankie."

"Let me."

She melts under my touch, just a little bit, and I take that as assent, pulling her gently through the crowd. People who witnessed my outburst watch us as they dance, and Sam's mild protestations drift to my ears, but I don't let any of it stop me, especially with the sharpness of the nails of her eager fingers pressing into my palm.

There's only one person in the large unisex bathroom when I pull her inside, adjusting his binder in the mirror. He stops when he sees us, smirks, and lets his shirt drop back down as he steps around us and out the door.

"Frankie—"

It's the only word she gets out before I push her up against a sink and devour her mouth. The taste of vodka on her tongue is all wrong, but the tart sweetness of orange juice is just so Sam, my Sam, or maybe it's all my Sam now. I pull her lower lip between my teeth and oh yes, that shuddering breath against my lips is definitely my girl's.

I kiss down to her throat while trailing my hands over her shoulders, skimming over her perfect little breasts on my way down to the curves of her waist. "So this is where the magic happens, huh?" she asks breathlessly.

"You'll have to tell me," I tease, nibbling her collarbone, but judging by the groans she's working to stifle behind a bitten lip, I'm doing just fine.

"Christ, Frankie, we're in a public bathroom." But even as she protests, her hips fight to get closer.

"Uh huh." I had no idea how much I missed her body, the scent of her hair, the salty sweetness of her skin. I can't stop my hands from wandering, stroking every inch in my reach.

"I might have overestimated how much Frankie I can handle," she says on a gasp as my thumb finds her nipple through her little indigo dress.

"I think you're underestimating how hard you're about to be fucked." Beneath the hem, she's so wet you'd think I'd been licking her thighs. I push the drenched fabric of her panties aside and slide two fingers inside her.

She cries out and grips the sink so hard her knuckles turn white. The tight, wet heat of her rocking into my hand is infuckingcredible, and I can't help but notice any trace of protest is gone.

"Still want me to stop?" I murmur in her ear.

"Don't you fucking dare." She grabs my forearm as if I'd even consider taking it back against her wishes, grinding so furiously on my hand that I forget I'm doing the fucking rather than being fucked. All I want is to hear that desperate gasp, the way she whimpers my name. I want to bury myself in every soft nook of her body. I want her passion and her caring and her low, melodious drawl. I want the sunshine she exudes from her skin.

I want *her*. Every fucking part.

It's with this thought that I press the heel of my hand into her clit until she comes, hard and hot all over my hand while she bites my shoulder to keep her cries quiet. Without even missing a beat, she grabs my ass to pull me against her, sliding her thigh between mine and sucking my throat as I ride her until I come too, taking no such measure to keep silent.

We take a minute to catch our breath, stifling laughter as a couple of guys walk in. "Okay," she says, smoothing her dress down. "You're making a decent argument for the Francesca Bellisario lifestyle."

"Right?"

She laughs. "Don't hold me to that. I won't be able to think coherently for the next hour. But"—she cups my chin and pulls me close for a kiss—"I'm not crazy about the fact that your clothes are still on. That seems like a serious flaw in this plan." She drops her voice to that low roll that caresses me everywhere like her rough, silky tongue. "Plus, you taste way better than vodka."

"Bad girl," I murmur against her lips. "Maybe you're more like me than we thought."

She hooks a finger into my belt loop, her knuckles grazing the bare skin at my waist. "I think maybe I've changed a little, too. And I'm pretty happy about it."

"I think changing together is not the worst thing."

"I think you are very wise."

"I think it's time to go back to my apartment and get you out of that dress, sweetheart."

She smiles against my lips. "Have I mentioned you are very wise?"

I press a hard kiss to her mouth and take her hand in mine. "Let's go and I'll have you screaming that in about twenty minutes."

• • •

Getting off in the bathroom sustains me for maybe half the ride back to my apartment, but between her arms wrapped around my waist, her tits pressed against my back, and her perfume floating on the breeze, I'm so keyed up by the time we pull up to the building that I nearly fall off the Vespa in my rush to get inside. The second I slam the door shut behind us, I push her up against it and attack her mouth with mine, and we grab at each other's clothing with a fierceness that makes it a wonder nothing rips. I'd been afraid I was too insatiable to settle down with one person, but if anything, I'm even more insatiable when it comes to her. I can't even imagine getting enough of this girl, can't imagine wanting to stop—

"Uh, guys?"

Unless it turned out we accidentally have an audience. I pull away from Sam with a sigh and slowly turn around to see Lizzie and Connor on the couch, gawking at us. Connor smoothly slides a throw pillow onto his lap.

"Oh, God, I'm so sorry." Even in the dimly lit room I can see Sam's face flaming red, and I grin.

"Please, don't let Lizzie give you shit. She's seen way worse."

"Yeah, well, my boyfriend's not quite highly evolved enough to be immune to the sight of two hot girls going at it, so."

"Elizabeth."

"I'm just gonna wait in your room." Sam dashes past me and slams the door behind her.

"I think I'll follow her lead," says Connor, disappearing into Lizzie's room.

"You'd think our significant others would be far more brazen by now," I muse to Lizzie.

"Significant, huh?" Lizzie straightens her shirt and curls her legs under her butt. "So you're all in now? Finally?"

I think of Samara—my girlfriend—lying on the other side of the wall. How I can't wait to touch and taste her again, to see what lingerie she's wearing. How I know that we'll both come again tonight, sure, but we'll laugh plenty too. How someday we'll make lasagna together, and choereg, but lots of nights will just be pad Thai or pizza on the couch, and that'll be perfect too. How there's still so much I want to learn about her, but so much I already know. How I worried this was going to be the end of who I am and instead it feels like a beginning.

"I'm all in now," I confirm. "Finally."

• • •

I can't help hoping I'll open the door to Sam lying on my bed in lingerie—or nothing at all—but no such luck; she's fully clothed, pacing across the floor. Doesn't matter; we'll get there.

"Hey," I say softly.

She stops pacing. "So, that was painfully embarrassing."

I smile. "You've heard the story of how Connor and Lizzie got caught, right? Trust me, that was nothing."

She tips her head. "Fair point." Then she finally relaxes into a smile too.

This should be the point where we meet in the middle and fall back on the bed and live happily ever after, but before all that begins, I know I need to ask her the question that's been plaguing me since I found her wrapped in a blanket on my couch. If I don't, I'll always worry about it happening again, and if I'm going to do this—for real—I need the last of my doubts soothed. "Can I ask you something?"

"Of course."

I take a deep breath. "Why did you really break up with me that morning?"

"I didn't b—"

"Yeah, you did, and you know it. Why?"

She levels me with a stare, and the little spark in her eyes makes me shiver. "You know why."

"Tell me."

252

She drops onto the bed, bracing her palms on her thighs. "Because I realized I had completely fallen for you."

Christ, those words...and saying them to me from my bed, smoky-smelling hair in her eyes, and coming from those kiss-swollen lips...fuck. "I thought that was the whole point."

"The point was to fall for each other. And when you didn't show up, I assumed that meant my feelings weren't mutual. But I told myself it doesn't matter, that I was putting too much pressure on this, and on sex. I thought if I showed up here, ready to go no matter what it meant, I could be detached about it, just like you are."

"*Were*," I bite out. "Before you."

Her delicious lips curve up at the corner. "Right. Anyway, I tried. It didn't work. From the second you put me in front of that mirror, I knew it wouldn't. Not because that is hands-down the hottest move I have ever seen in my entire life—though it is—but because I knew I would do anything you told me to."

"Sam—"

"I don't mean I can't think for myself or because you pressured me," she clarifies, and I feel a tension slipping from my shoulders I hadn't even realized had been gathering. "I mean because I trusted you so fully and completely. I have never felt that with another person, Frankie. I have spent years in fear of how my friends and family will react when they find out all of who I really am. But you already knew, and you looked at me like...God, I don't know. You make me feel perfect, exactly as I am."

Inside my chest, my heart is cracking into a thousand tiny pieces, and all those pieces are furiously making out with each other. I can't even muster words, just a nod in agreement that yes, that is exactly how I see her.

"I was so terrified of that feeling. Because to be the only one in a relationship who feels it? I couldn't. I couldn't let myself feel like *that* and be alone in it."

"You weren't," I manage around the lump in my throat. "I swear on everything I have, you weren't."

"And now I know that," she says, rising, "so I'm here."

She is. The girl who knows exactly who I am—has always known—and loves me anyway.

No, not "anyway." Just straight-up loves me.

I watch her walk toward me, slow and sinuous and mindfuckingly beautiful, and when she's close enough to feel the words on her lips, I say, "I love you." I always thought saying those words to someone for the first time would feel like a surrender, but they don't. And when she smiles and says, "I love you, too," I realize that somewhere along the way, this most terrifying thing became the best kind of foreplay.

She's got fingers hooked into my belt loops to hold me close, and her mouth on mine is a delightfully teasing thing—slow strokes of her tongue, gently nipping teeth, barely there brushes against my lips that nearly bring me to begging. I'm about to kiss her for real when she says, "Now I have a question."

I have to stifle a frustrated cry because I am fucking throbbing, but I got to ask my question, and she certainly gets hers. "What is it?"

"When you called me from New York, were you…?" She trails off, blushing fiercely, and underneath skin-tight denim, a useless scrap of fabric drowns.

"Was I what?" I ask innocently.

"Frankie."

"Samara."

"Frankie."

"Ask your question," I say as coolly as I can manage considering the look in her eyes is liquid fire.

Her gaze just barely slips off mine. "Fine. Were you…touching yourself when you were talking to me on the phone?"

She says the words so quickly that if I weren't in a state to hydrate the Sahara, I would've laughed. "Let's say I was. Is that bad?"

She shakes her head, swallowing loudly, and I love that she can still be teased like this, less than an hour after being fucked in a public bathroom. Still so much innocence in there.

Or at least I thought so, but then she rasps, "Show me."

Jesus fucking Christ. Now I'm the one feeling shy. I've done a lot of stuff with a lot of people, but not that. Not in person.

But with the way she's looking at me right now? No way in hell I'm saying no.

I place a hand on her shoulder and walk her slowly back to the bed until her thighs hit the mattress and she's forced to sit. Then I drop my fingers to the button of my jeans and keep my eyes on her as she watches me undo it as torturously slowly as I can. We're so close her breath is tickling my hand as I move to my zipper and lower it at glacial speed. Then I abandon my jeans to stroke and tease my way down the silken fabric of my low-cut top until I hit the waistband of the pink-lace-edged thong peeking out, and stop.

"I think it's only fair you give me something to look at." I brush the little strip of skin just above the lace with a fingertip, and judging by the breath she sucks in through her teeth, she's at least as tortured by the motion as I am.

She recovers quickly, though. Her lips curve into a sly smile and she says, "Fair enough." She moves back on the bed and rises to her knees, then pulls her dress over her head in one smooth motion.

My hand freezes. "Mother of God."

"Will this work?" she asks innocently.

"This" is a corset-panty set, completely sheer save for intricate, strategically placed embroidery of black vines and roses that snakes around her lithe form and begs in a moan to be touched. "Let's find out," I utter, unable to resist for another second.

I dare say it doesn't surprise either of us when I shudder the second a single fingertip brushes my clit.

"Guessing that's a yes," she murmurs, then slides back on the bed until she's up against my pillows, watching and waiting. I push my jeans down to the floor and pull the top over my head, far too impatient now for a full-on strip tease, and crawl over her until I'm straddling her waist.

Then I dip my hand down below again.

"Frankie." My name is nothing but a breath.

"Mm?"

"This." She hooks a finger into my thong and slides it down just an inch, her fingertips sizzling my skin where they graze it. "The last one."

"Told you you'd find it eventually."

"Fuck, that's hot," she murmurs, placing a kiss right over the black ink reading *Mine*. "Now get back to work."

I'm so fucking aroused my clit may as well be a land mine, and neither Sam's hands holding me upright by cupping my ass nor her smoldering gaze as she watches me is doing anything to cool me down.

"Is this what you had in mind?" I ask, slipping a finger inside, just up to the first knuckle, knowing she can tell exactly what's happening through the thin lace of my thong.

She shakes her head slowly. "You are always so, so far beyond what I can even imagine. Nothing I can conjure in my head ever compares."

"But you *do* conjure me in your head," I can't resist saying.

"Frankie." She gently pulls my hand free, her gaze holding mine as she takes my wet fingertip into her mouth. "I do *everything* to you in my head."

"Jesus, Samara Jane, do you fuck your girlfriend with that mouth?"

She tugs my lip between her teeth. "Only when she's good."

Holy fuck, this girl. I can't take another breath without kissing her, so I do, over and over until I don't even know whose tongue is whose anymore. "Doesn't seem like either of us is being very good tonight," I murmur against her lips. "So maybe you should tell me what you want, my newly minted bad girl."

She smiles and takes my face in her hands. "Know what I want?" Another kiss, this one gentle against my lips. "I want you to fuck me like you don't know you're the only person I've ever been with."

"I *don't* know that," I point out, sliding my finger just inside the panty string spanning her hip. "You're the one who's been dating around while I've been taking care of myself all over my apartment."

"Oh come on," she says, her voice barely above a whisper as she skates her hands up my ribcage and palms my breasts. "You didn't seriously think I hooked up with anyone, did you? Frankie, I can't even look at myself in a full-length mirror without thinking about being with you." She unhooks my strapless bra and tosses it to the floor. "For as wild as I like to think I've become"—she punctuates her sentence with a swirl of her tongue around my nipple that sends goose bumps over my entire body—"only you do this to me." She sucks my other nipple into her mouth, sending my eyes rolling back into my head. "Only you make me feel like I can do absolutely anything."

"You definitely can," I say on a groan. "Especially that."

She smiles against my skin and sucks again, harder, and my hips respond by pressing back equally hard, fabric rubbing against fabric, so close to what I want, what I need, but not quite there. I sit back and slide my finger back inside that string. "I think it's time for this to go."

There's no argument from her as we part just long enough for me to slide her underwear down her legs, and her to do the same to me. Then she turns to present me her back, where the corset dips low into a line of complicated little hooks. I groan as I start to unfasten them, and find that my clumsy, far-too-eager fingers can't do a damn thing. I kiss the top of her spine and give up. "This will have to stay. Get back here."

She turns back to me and I waste no time climbing back on top of her and covering her mouth with mine, straddling her until wet, naked flesh rubs wet naked flesh and ignites me with hot, desperate need. I fuck her like I don't know I'm the only person she's ever been with, and I fuck her like I know she's the only person I wanna be with, and we both come so hard I swear the earth must be shifting beneath us. It feels like hours before I can even open my eyes, but when I do, there she is, right next to me, my girlfriend, my girlfriend, my girl.

"Good news," Sam says, tucking a piece of sweaty hair behind my ear when we can finally breathe again.

"What's that?"

"I am definitely gay."

I laugh and kiss her shoulder, her cheek, her lips. "Phew. I know that was touch-'n-go there for a little while. Glad it turned out to be touch-'n-come instead."

"Oh my God, Frankie, that was horrible."

"I'm sorry, it really was." But I can't help grinning anyway. "Still like me?"

"Questionable."

"Still love me?"

"Possibly even more so."

I reach between us for her hand and squeeze it. "Most important question, though, my book-loving girl—do you ship us?"

"How could I *not* ship us?"

"But, like, where do we rank? Do we beat Tim and Jenna?"

"You mean Taylor and Jonah?" She sighs. "Yes, Frankie, I ship us harder than Taylor and Jonah."

"What about those books where you switched teams from one guy to the other in the middle? The one where you said the pink-covered book almost turned you bi."

She contemplates for a minute. "I ship us harder than the girl with either guy," she says carefully.

"But not more than if they were a threesome."

"I mean...come on."

"Fair. What about—"

She places a finger over my lips. "There's no competition, Francesca. I don't know what I want to do about my family, and I don't know what I'm actually gonna do with this degree and...God, there is a lot I don't know. But you are the first thing in my life that's ever been exactly what *I* want. So as long as you'll stick by me while I figure it all out, we are my OTP forever and ever."

"Your O-what?"

She sighs. "Shut up and kiss me."

"If I follow your instructions, does that make me a good girl?"

"It might have if you'd done it."

"Touché." But I shut up and kiss her anyway, because I want to, and because I need to prove that I can be good when she needs me to be—that I *will* be, as she figures the rest of this stuff out. Maybe I've officially earned her and maybe I haven't, but I think part of loving someone is that you never stop trying either way.

Our kisses become lazier as we both grow sleepy, and I finally help her out of that corset so she can get comfortable. As I curl around her to pull her close and cover us with a blanket, I get a little pang in my chest as I remember the last time we fell asleep together. "Hey," I whisper into her ear. "You'll be here when I wake up, right?"

Under the blanket, she wraps her fingers around mine. "I'm not going anywhere this time. I promise." She brings our hands to her lips and kisses my knuckles. "What about you? If I make a reservation for that restaurant for tomorrow night, will you be there?"

"With bells on. No promises about pants."

She sighs and pulls our arms around her waist. "So this is what I'm committing to, huh?"

"Gotta take the bad with the good, Sam. It's what keeps life interesting."

I can practically feel her roll her eyes, but she snuggles into me anyway, and it's all the response I need. Yeah, the tiniest part of me still finds the prospect of a serious relationship scary. And the tiniest part of me is worried I'll still freak out sometimes. And I know that not everything will always feel as perfect as it does right now. And I know there's bound to be some shit ahead.

But right now, I'm falling into a peaceful sleep, and I'm as happy as I've ever been, in a way I never knew I could be. I spend every day in that studio or at my easel or sketchpad trying to capture and create beauty that pales in comparison to the girl in my arms right now. And if I had to interpret Hope again, I know I'd paint it a lot like this.

Possibly with more clothing, but probably not.

epilogue

end of junior year

Frankieeee!! Hurry up!!!

Chill, Lizzie B, I text back. *The more you make me stop to respond to you, the slower I'm gonna go.* I know that'll shut her up, so I shove my phone back into the pocket of my cutoffs and continue my last-chance survey of the apartment before leaving for the summer.

The place is completely full of shit. Cait, Connor, Mase, and Sam all live in dorms, so whatever's not coming with them now—bedding, winter clothes, and unspeakable amounts of assorted crap—is lying all over our apartment. But I like the mess, if I'm being honest. It feels like a promise that we'll all be back. That we'll return the same found family unit we've been working our way into from the day Cait, Lizzie, and I were placed together through the six months and counting Samara's been putting up with me.

I mentally tick off everything important I might be forgetting. As many art supplies as I could cram into the car Lizzie's graciously lending me for the trip? Check. Socks, because for some reason, Lizzie and Connor insist we must hit a certain bowling alley on our caravan's way down to Pomona? Check. Ample amounts of sunscreen for lying around on various beaches on the way south, mostly to give me an excuse to rub my hands all over Samara's bikini body? Definite check.

The caravan was Lizzie's idea—one epic journey to say goodbye as we split for the summer. It's a five-hour drive from Radleigh down to her house in Pomona, where we'll be dropping her and Connor off to stay with her brothers for the summer, and the two of them have somehow managed to find a billion things for us to do along the way. Then the remaining four of us will continue on to Philly so "Claw" can spend a little time with Mase's mom and brother before Cait starts her summer job at a bank.

And then, finally, it'll just be me and Samara, ambling down toward South Carolina, toward Meridian, toward what she may be calling home for the last time.

I've told her a million times she doesn't have to tell them anything she's not ready for, but she says if we can survive driving all the way from Upstate New York to South Carolina together, then I'm clearly someone her family and friends need to know about. So that's our new deal: we make it down there, we make it everywhere.

I feel pretty damn good about our chances.

As if she can tell I'm thinking about her, she calls me right then, "S&M" muffled by my denim pocket. I pull out my phone and allow myself to appreciate the picture of her lighting up my screen—the way her eyes are sparkling and her skin is glowing and her smile is teasing and all of it is because I'm the one behind the camera, taking her (secretly post-coital) picture.

Hell, I feel pretty fucking good about everything.

"Hey, you."

"Frankie, you've got to get out here. Lizzie's trying to get me to send you topless photos to lure you out."

"So if I stay here, I get boob shots?"

Sam sighs. "Trust me, Cait and Connor are practically fistfighting over which one gets to explain to her how incentives actually work."

"I'll be out in a minute, I swear."

"Is everything okay?"

"Yeah, yeah, just being a sap. I'm appreciating that this will be the last summer break that *isn't* followed by everything in the world changing."

"Maybe everything in the world won't change after graduation either," says Sam. "Mase graduated, and he's still coming back for another year."

"Yeah, but for a master's and to keep coaching. We already know neither of us has grad school plans right now, and Cait will work at a bank or something for a few years before business school, and Lizzie's gonna move back and get custody of her brothers for good, and Connor's done here after one more year, and—"

"Oh my God, Frankie, breathe." Her gentle laughter floats through the phone line. "I've never heard you get so nostalgic."

"Me neither," I admit. "There's a lot to miss about this place, I guess."

"Well, you don't have to start missing it for a long time, so why don't you get that sexy ass out here and actually hang out with us?"

She has a point. "Fine, but I'm instituting a rest stop-makeout rule."

"Deal."

Finally, the nervous tingles that've been coursing through my body all day are replaced by ones of anticipation. "Okay, I'm coming."

"Not yet, you're not," she drawls, "but I bet we can fix that somewhere around Binghamton."

Have I mentioned I fucking love this girl?

I head outside and the others make exaggerated "Finally!" proclamations while I flip them off, gliding straight over to Samara for a kiss.

"I had a feeling she'd be able to lure you out," Cait says with a wink.

"So confident in yourself now that you're a two-time national champion." I stick my tongue out at her. "You're not the boss of *me*, Captain Johannssen."

She just beams smugly in response, while Mase drops a kiss into her hair. Her new title has totally gone to her head, and the rest of us couldn't be prouder.

"Enough, children!" Lizzie claps her hands. "We're already running behind schedule. Get in your cars!"

"So, she's always this bossy, huh?" Mase murmurs to Connor.

"Yes, yes she is," Connor replies under his breath, as if we don't all know he's completely turned-on by it.

But none of us want to face Lizzie's wrath, so we get in our cars like the relatively well-behaved students we are.

And off we go.

acknowledgments

Finishing a series is a bittersweet thing. When the last four words of this book came to me as I was walking down the street, I'm not ashamed to admit I teared up. The Radleigh University books are, by definition, Romances, but for me—and I'd venture to say for most readers—the friendship between Lizzie, Cait, and Frankie is the heart of the series, and I will miss these girls unspeakable amounts. First and foremost, my deepest thanks to anyone reading this, for sharing them with me, for caring about the Radleigh girls (almost) as much as I do.

Of course, nothing inspires fictional friendship like the friends who get you through the day in the real world. To that end, my deepest love and gratitude to:

Lindsay Smith, who whips my butt into shape, champions everything I do, and picks me back up when I don't do it all that well; Katie Locke, who…I feel like I should just text this all to you instead, as we generally realize about most things; Marieke Nijkamp, who somehow holds my hand through so many things from across an ocean, and Maggie Hall, who does it from across a continent; Sara Taylor Woods and Rick Lipman, who complete the rainbow tribe of my heart; Gina Ciocca, who will always be my bookish fam, and whose real-life fam has welcomed me with such open arms; my West Coast Bae, Candice Montgomery, whom I love despite being so superhumanly talented and helpful, she makes me feel bad about my everything; Patricia Riley, who will forever be my editor in life in one way or another; Ashley Herring Blake, who I'll be quiet about now because I won't shut up about her in 2017; Becky Albertalli, who probably carries more kindness in her pinky than most people give in a lifetime; my sister-mods, Jess, Sharon, Kelly, and Tess, who are the most wonderful little family in the world; and all the gif-bearing darlings of my Twittering heart—you know who you are.

To the women of NA Hideaway, I don't know WTF I would do without you. Thank you for being brilliant, for sharing your wisdom, for endless support, for the most ridiculous laughs, and for hugs both virtual and otherwise as needed.

Thank you to those who made this particular book shine—to Ashley, Cam, Patricia, Chelsea, and Jenn for your wonderful beta notes; Katie, for your early edits; Sarah, my copyediting queen; Cait, for magically making my books look like books (and being so excited for this one); and Maggie, who creates such perfect covers I wish I could wallpaper my entire world in them. Many thanks, too, to Louisse Ang, Charliene Paule, and Karla from Reads and Thoughts, for your much-appreciated assistance in this book's Filipino menu planning!

Thank you so much to the incredible, selfless readers, bloggers, and authors who've supported my books all along the way. I'm so blessed to be surrounded by people who love books as much as I do, and who squeeze mine into their massive TBRs, and who are just wonderful besides, including but in no way limited to Christina, Debby, Natasha, Chasia, Sil, Ashley, Marie, Jim, Shelly, Anna, Emilie, Serena, Jessica, Bekka, Angie, Shira, Alexandra, Lauren, and, of course, Dahl's Den of Iniquity.

To all my friends and family who quietly support me, who step outside their comfort zones to read my words—thank you. I love you. Let's never speak of this again.

And to Yoni, with love and gratitude and my whole heart, always.

about the author

Dahlia Adler is an Associate Editor of Mathematics by day, a blogger for the B&N Teen Blog and LGBTQ Reads by night, and writes Contemporary YA and NA at every spare moment in between. She's the author of the Daylight Falls series, *Just Visiting*, and the Radleigh University series, and she lives in New York City with her husband and their overstuffed bookshelves. If you give her a macaron, she just might fall in love with you.

More often than not, you can find her on Twitter as @MissDahlELama, and on her blog, the Daily Dahlia.

Turn the page to see how it all began in Book #1 of the Radleigh University series,

last will and

TESTAMENT

chapter one

Supposedly no one even answered the front door when they first started knocking. No one could hear it over the music blasting from the speakers, the Sigma Psi Omegas chanting around keg stands, and Jessica Fiorello singing loudly along with some song no one else seemed to hear. (She got admitted to the hospital that night for alcohol poisoning, but nobody really talks about that. It kinda got lost in what came next. Lucky me.)

I didn't hear the knocking either. The tightly closed door of Trevor Matlin's room made sure of that. Even if it hadn't, Trevor's moaning in my ear as he begged me to get down on my knees probably would've drowned it out. He's never been very quiet. Kinda makes me wonder how we got away with it for so long.

The knocking was impossible to miss when it sounded on Trevor's door, though. And once Trev and I were silenced by it, it was almost as easy to hear Sophie Springer yelling, "Why the hell would you think she's in there? That's my boyfriend's room."

"Shit," Trevor mutters, yanking his pants back up as I straighten myself out. "Who the hell is that?"

"Well *I* obviously don't know," I whisper back, snatching my black-framed glasses from his nightstand and sliding them on. "Am I zipped?" I show him the back of my sleeveless top, then check my fly.

"Yeah," he says. "Me?"

"Yeah. Wait, no, your buttons are off."

"Trevor Matlin? Are you in there?"

"Who wants to know?" he calls back as we both scramble to fix his shirt.

"This is the Radleigh Police Department. We're looking for Elizabeth Brandt. We have reason to believe she may be with you."

Trevor and I both freeze, eyes widening in a panic. "Why the fuck are the cops after you?" he whispers fiercely.

"I have no idea! Just tell them I'm not here."

"I can't lie to the cops!"

"Your girlfriend is standing right outside that door," I remind him. I have no love for Sophie Springer—not since she "accidentally" spilled her beer on me last year when she spotted me talking to Trevor for the first time—but that doesn't mean I want her seeing me with her boyfriend, in the flesh.

As if on cue, Sophie yells, "That slut better not be in there, Trevor Matlin!"

"Ma'am, please," I hear an officer say, his voice muffled. I wonder how many of them there are. What the hell are the police doing after me? I wouldn't say I'm a model citizen, but they just walked through an entire house of underage drinkers, so…. Then the same officer says, "Mr. Matlin, I'm not going to ask again. Open this door."

Trev and I exchange one more quick glance and then I dash under the bed, squeezing in as much of my body as possible. I'm not tiny, but sadly, this isn't my first time in a similar predicament, though this *is* the first time the cops are involved. I've learned how to get decent coverage under Trevor's full-size mattress.

I pull the blanket down enough to cover me but still allow me to see feet, just as Trevor pulls open the door. "Sorry about that," Trevor says with the same charismatic smoothness that allows him to be president of Sigma Psi Omega, date the campus princess, and bang a random nobody on the side. "How can I help you, officers?"

"We're looking for Elizabeth Brandt," one of them replies. I count shoes. Six, including Trev's. They're all men's, but I know Sophie's lurking there somewhere. I can feel her silent fuming. "Her roommate said she was probably here with you."

Fucking Cait.

"Sorry, officer—I don't even know who that is, or why her roommate thinks she'd be here."

"That's what I've been trying to tell them," Sophie says, her voice steel-edged.

"Are you certain about that, son?" the other officer asks. "It's very important we speak with her."

"Very certain," Trevor says. Hell, I'd believe him with that confidence in his voice, if I didn't know way, way better. "I'm sorry I can't help you gentlemen. Whatever this girl did, I hope you catch her."

"She didn't do anything, Mr. Matlin. There's been a family emergency. If you find—"

I whoosh out from under the bed like a tidal wave; I'll deal with Sophie later. "What family emergency?" I demand, getting to my feet on wobbly legs. "What happened?"

The officers don't even look amused at the fact that they've caught perfect Trevor Matlin cheating on perfect Sophie Springer, and that's when I know this is really, really bad. My brain starts to go fuzzy and my hands clam up, my heart turning over in my chest. Sophie's screeching at Trevor somewhere in the room, but it's barely penetrating my consciousness.

"Elizabeth Brandt?"

"Yeah. Yes, I mean. That's me. But…Lizzie. It's Lizzie." My tongue feels enormous as it struggles to work with my lips and teeth to form words.

"Lizzie." The lighter-haired officer's face falls, and I can tell he's wishing I'd never slid out from under that bed, that he'd never found me at all. "I'm so sorry. There's been a terrible accident. Your parents…they didn't make it. I'm so sorry."

I know the words he's saying are horrible, life-altering ones, but I can't seem to assign them any meaning right now. Because he can't be saying what I think he's saying. I wonder if it's his first time delivering news like this. It certainly sounds like it is. The double apology—that's the giveaway. He's new at this, new to the force. Looks it, too, all young and covered in shaving nicks.

"Lizzie?" I'm not even sure who says my name. It might be one of the officers. It might be Trevor. Hell, it might even be Sophie. I'm so far away, I swear it could be fucking Santa Claus. I shouldn't have had those stupid Jell-O shots. They're just confusing everything right now.

"Lizzie?"

"Miss Brandt?"

I blink. I'm not sure why it's "Miss Brandt" that does it, but it is. "I'm sorry, did you just say that my parents are dead?"

"Yes, Ma'am. I'm so sorry."

"You apologize a lot."

"I'm sorry."

I smile, just a little, and it briefly occurs to me I must look deranged. I *feel* deranged. "You're still doing it."

"Miss Brandt—"

"Please don't call me that." I hold up a hand. "My parents are dead. Yes? That's what's happening here? That's *actually* what you meant to say?"

"Yes."

It feels like I've swallowed a blade and it is slowly but surely shredding my insides with every word. "My parents were in an accident, and they were alive, and now they're dead. My parents, like, the people who raised me. Edward and Manuella Brandt. Tall lawyer guy with a mustache? Filipina high school history teacher? Those parents?"

"Miss Brandt—"

"*It's Lizzie.*"

"Lizzie, then. Do you have a counselor on campus? Someone you can speak to? A family member we can reach out to?"

It's like having salt rubbed in an open wound the size of my entire chest cavity. "Didn't you just tell me my parents are dead? Who the fuck in my family would I want to reach out to if my parents are dead?"

Blondie wants to melt into the floor; I can see it. I should feel bad, I know, but also, apparently my parents are dead, and I don't give a fuck how he feels.

"We've spoken to your grandmother—"

"Fantastic. She won't remember in the morning."

"And your aunt—"

"Well, I'm sure that stopped her drinking for a whole thirty seconds."

Dark Hair sighs again. They really should've introduced themselves. If you're going to tell an eighteen-year-old college sophomore that her parents are dead, don't you think you should at least open with an "I'm Officer So-and-So" first? "Yes, we gathered that the rest of your family is... not in a position to assist you with this news. Is there anyone else?"

And then it hits me like an actual punch to the gut. Of course there's someone else. There are two someone elses. "My brothers," I whisper. "Where are my brothers? Are my brothers okay?"

"Your brothers are being taken care of," Blondie assures me, confident again now that he actually has something to offer other than my name and an apology. "Your neighbor has them right now. We're working on other arrangements."

"But...permanently. Who...? What...?" I don't even know what I should be asking. This is an insane amount to process for someone who *isn't* half-drunk and wasn't interrupted mid-sex haze, let alone me, right now. "I need to sit."

I forgot Trevor was even standing there, but suddenly, he gets his ass in gear and brings me a chair. I drop into it like a lead weight.

"Miss Brandt—Lizzie—your brothers will ultimately need to be cared for by a long-term guardian, whom your parents have presumably designated. Once you're with your family, a lawyer and a social worker will help you through this difficult time."

But I stopped listening after "guardian." Because I know exactly who my parents designated. And it's someone who can barely handle her own life, let alone that of a thirteen- and seven-year-old.

"Me," I blurt out. "It's me. I'm their guardian now. I'm the one in the will."

The officers exchange a look. "If you, and a judge, feel that you're equipped to serve in that capacity." It's pretty clear from their demeanors that they possess no such feeling about me.

"And what happens if I—we—don't?"

"You really should talk to your lawyer and social worker, Miss Brandt," says Dark Hair.

"It's going to be a little while before I get to do that, considering I don't have either one right now." Is someone reaching into my skull and squeezing my brain? It really feels like it. But at least discussing logistics is keeping me from losing it outright. "Please just tell me what you know. Generally."

"Generally, either they'll go to another family member—"

"I think we've already established that won't be happening."

"Or they'll enter foster care," Dark Hair finishes.

"No."

"No, what?"

"No, you're not making my brothers into foster children. They're my brothers. I'll do it. I'll take care of them. I can. I promise." This is sort of a lie, but it's all I can say right then.

"Lizzie, come on," says Trevor.

"Fuck you, Trevor. No one asked you." I turn back to the officers. "How does this work? What happens now? When can I see them?"

"First, let's get you back to your room," says Blondie, shooting a glare at Trevor. "We can talk there, or you can come to the station."

"Yeah, sure, whatever." I've had enough of Trevor's room anyway. I need to get out. I need to breathe fresh air. "Let's go."

I'd completely forgotten that there was an entire frat party taking place in the house until I followed the officers downstairs and found myself being stared at by every single resident of Greek Row. It's hard to tell what people know; some faces are disgusted, some sympathetic, and some are just curious. I focus on the back of Blondie's head as we walk out the door. It isn't exactly how I'd imagined my first time in a police cruiser would be, but there really isn't anything about this night I'd pictured happening as it does.

Only when we pull away from the house, and Trevor and Sophie are gone, and I can hear the music blast from the house once again, do I fall apart in the backseat and cry.

Made in the USA
Lexington, KY
23 June 2016